KU-218-645

Seeing her again at the party had brought back with a vengeance all the anger he had experienced, the disappointment, the fear that she might never have truly loved him, had simply married him for the lifestyle he could give her.

Even then she hadn't been satisfied, he thought bitterly. She really did deserve to be hurt as much as she had hurt him. Revenge was going to be very sweet indeed.

But one step at a time.

He saw her brace herself; he saw her struggling with emotion. 'I couldn't work for you. Not again.'

Hunter allowed himself a small smile. 'Maybe you need time to think it over?'

The thought of revenge gave him great pleasure. There was only one fly in the ointment. Today he had felt a faint surge of feeling for her. Nothing much, but enough to warn him to be on his guard. He could be wrong, of course. He hoped he was wrong. He wanted nothing that would ruin his grand plan.

Margaret Mayo was reading Mills & Boon® romances long before she began to write them. In fact she never had any plans to become a writer. After an idea for a short story popped into her head she was thrilled when it turned into a full-scale novel. Now, over twenty-five years later, she is still happily writing and says she has no intention of stopping. She lives with her husband Ken in a rural part of Staffordshire, England. She has two children: Adrian, who now lives in America, and Tina. Margaret's hobbies are reading, photography, and more recently watercolour painting, which she says has honed her observational skills and is a definite advantage when it comes to writing.

Recent titles by the same author:

THE RICH MAN'S RELUCTANT MISTRESS
BOUGHT FOR MARRIAGE
AT THE SPANIARD'S CONVENIENCE

BEDDED AT HIS CONVENIENCE

BY

MARGARET MAYO

MILLS & BOON®

DID YOU PURCHASE THIS BOOK WITHOUT A COVER?

If you did, you should be aware it is **stolen property** as it was reported *unsold and destroyed* by a retailer. Neither the author nor the publisher has received any payment for this book.

All the characters in this book have no existence outside the imagination of the author, and have no relation whatsoever to anyone bearing the same name or names. They are not even distantly inspired by any individual known or unknown to the author, and all the incidents are pure invention.

All Rights Reserved including the right of reproduction in whole or in part in any form. This edition is published by arrangement with Harlequin Enterprises II BV/S.à.r.l. The text of this publication or any part thereof may not be reproduced or transmitted in any form or by any means, electronic or mechanical, including photocopying, recording, storage in an information retrieval system, or otherwise, without the written permission of the publisher.

This book is sold subject to the condition that it shall not, by way of trade or otherwise, be lent, resold, hired out or otherwise circulated without the prior consent of the publisher in any form of binding or cover other than that in which it is published and without a similar condition including this condition being imposed on the subsequent purchaser.

MILLS & BOON and MILLS & BOON with the Rose Device are registered trademarks of the publisher.

First published in Great Britain 2007
Harlequin Mills & Boon Limited,
Eton House, 18-24 Paradise Road, Richmond, Surrey TW9 1SR

© Margaret Mayo 2007

ISBN-13: 978 0263 85345 2

Set in Times Roman 10½ on 12¾ pt
01-0807-50223

Printed and bound in Spain
by Litografia Rosés, S.A., Barcelona

BEDDED AT HIS CONVENIENCE

CHAPTER ONE

'I CAN'T GO to a party!' declared Keisha firmly, glaring at her friend. 'I have nothing to wear. Nor do I have any money. And I'm about to be thrown out of my house. Why are you asking me?'

'Because it's exactly what you need,' insisted Gillian, her voice firm. 'You've been out of the social circle for far too long.'

'And I'm in no position to enter it again,' countered Keisha, green eyes flashing her irritation that Gillian had even thought about asking her.

But Gillian ignored her friend's denial. 'You can borrow one of my dresses.'

At one time the other woman's clothes wouldn't have fitted her, but the pounds had dropped off Keisha during the last three years. Gone were her voluptuous curves, and instead she was painfully thin. With her pale complexion and long ash-blonde hair, Keisha sometimes thought that she looked like a wraith. 'I still don't want to go,' she maintained, her lips pressed firmly together.

'I'm relying on you,' retorted Gillian. 'No way am I going to sit in alone when there's a party to go to. Come on, we haven't been out together for ages. Please? Do it for me?'

Keisha smiled weakly, beginning to feel selfish. Gillian had been a good friend, and she had been looking forward to this party. Would it really hurt her to make the effort?

'OK, I'll go. But just for you!'

Arriving at the party later that evening, Keisha felt good for the first time in ages. Gillian had worked wonders with her appearance, styling her long blonde hair into a sophisticated chignon, and applying just the right amount of make-up to highlight Keisha's amazing eyes. Gillian had also made sure that Keisha wore something that flattered her thin frame, instead of drawing attention to her weight loss.

Slowly Keisha began to relax, and to enjoy herself. The last three years had been hard, and this party was exactly what she needed—time to have a bit of fun!

But as Keisha stood assessing the many glamorous people present at the party she quickly realised she had made a huge mistake. Standing on the other side of the room was Hunter Donahue. The blood drained from Keisha's face and she wanted to turn tail and run. But already it was too late. Narrowed eyes were fixed in her direction, and a frown was furrowing an already darkened brow. Keisha's stomach curled into a tight knot.

She turned to her friend, but Gillian was talking to someone else. When Keisha looked back in Hunter's direction she discovered, much to her relief, that he had disappeared.

Until a hand touched her shoulder!

She shivered, goosebumps standing out on her bare arms like corn stubble in a freshly harvested field.

'What are *you* doing here?'

Oh, that voice! That beautiful deep voice! Why did it still

have the power to send shivers of a very different kind through her? So many pleasures they had shared, so much excitement. But things had gone drastically wrong and she had fled their marriage three years ago. She hadn't seen him since.

She tried not to think about the great sex they'd shared—which was hard with someone as physically gorgeous as Hunter—lifting her chin instead, and looking coolly into the blue depths of his eyes.

Still beautiful eyes, she couldn't help thinking. Come-to-bed eyes. Eyes that had been used very much to his advantage! Oh, hell, why was she thinking like this when they were divorced?

'Who are you with?'

He didn't look too pleased to see her either, thought Keisha, although she couldn't help wondering whether he felt any of the old sparks—or whether she was the only one who remembered how fantastic those first months of marriage had been.

'Who is he?' Hunter's eyes scanned the crowded room as he persisted in finding out who her companion was.

The party was being held in one of London's top hotels. Keisha remembered Gillian telling her what it was in aid of, but for the life of her she couldn't remember why all these businessmen were gathered together.

'It isn't a he, it's a she,' Keisha answered. 'Do you have a problem with me being here?' She let her wide green eyes rest on his cool blue ones, her chin tilted as she looked up at him. He certainly didn't look pleased. In fact he looked as though she was the last person on earth he wanted to see again.

And she could hardly blame him when she was the one who'd done the walking.

'No, I don't have a problem,' he answered. 'I'm shocked,

I guess. You've changed, Keisha. You've lost weight. I hardly recognised you.'

She lifted her too-thin shoulders and let them drop again. 'I'm sure it's no concern of yours.'

Hunter, on the other hand, had put on a few pounds. Not too much, possibly all muscle—as though he still worked out on a daily basis. He looked good. Far too arresting for her peace of mind!

'On the contrary,' he said, much to her surprise, 'it is very much my concern. I'm interested in what you've been doing since you—deserted me.' He lifted her hand and made a show of studying it. 'No ring, I see. So you haven't married again?'

Keisha shook her head, snatching her hand free, alarmed at the flurry of feelings that his touch had triggered. Feelings that she had thought were dead. And had now learned were very much alive. Hunter, she was discovering, was not a man who could be dismissed easily.

If ever!

Keisha told herself that she was being ridiculous. Why couldn't she dismiss him? Their marriage had failed. They were divorced. He meant nothing to her any more.

'I don't suppose I can flatter myself that your loss of weight has anything to do with me?'

His devastating blue eyes looked deeply into hers and her throat tightened, pulses beginning to pound. She had run away because he'd neglected her, because he'd worked too hard and she'd rarely seen him—*and because he had been seeing another woman.*

Not because she had fallen out of love.

Three years was a long time. She ought to be over him. She had thought she was. And now she was shattered to discover that some of those feelings were still alive.

Keisha couldn't help wondering whether Hunter was experiencing any similar feelings. Lord help her if he was, because if he turned his fatal charm on her she wouldn't be able to resist. It had taken her but a few seconds to discover that.

Her only consolation was that she was older and wiser. She tossed her head and flashed her green eyes magnificently. 'As if!' And she took a step backwards.

Over Hunter's shoulder she saw Gillian glance in her direction. What she wouldn't give to call her friend over and suggest that they leave. But to do so would alert him to her unease, and that was the last thing she wanted. She needed to remain cool and aloof, and not let him see by even the flicker of an eyelash that he could still stir her senses.

Even though she'd always sworn as a young girl that she would never get married—her father had come and gone, finally disappearing into the ether when she was only nine, so her lasting impression of men was that they were never there when they were needed—she'd been totally bowled over by this man, by his softly spoken words and his eyes full of promise.

Keisha had left school at eighteen—there had been no money for university or higher education; she'd needed to earn a living. Her mother had suffered from bouts of depression ever since her husband had left and had never worked. Therefore Keisha had felt it her duty to get a job—even though she would have liked nothing better than to join her friends at university.

She'd found employment as an office junior at Hunter's advertising agency. Every female had been in love with the boss; even the guys had admired him. He'd had jet-black hair and dancing blue eyes, and the looks of a film star. Not that he'd seemed aware of it; he hadn't been big-headed or vain. Just totally at ease with himself.

When Keisha had dropped a folder full of papers he had helped her pick them up and she had been flattered. But when their eyes had locked momentarily she'd felt a thrill of something unexpected. And when, a couple of days later, he'd asked her out on a date she'd been overcome.

Of course she hadn't refused him; who would have? Even though she'd felt that he was out of her league! She had thought that it would be a one-off date, that he would quickly realise how young and immature she was. But it hadn't worked out like that. One date had followed another, followed swiftly by a proposal, and three months later, just after her nineteenth birthday, they'd been married.

It hadn't been a big flamboyant wedding, just a quiet ceremony in their local church. Her mother had bought herself a new outfit, and Keisha had worn a white satin dress that had fitted her like a dream. It had been a beautiful day from start to finish, the best in her life, and Keisha knew that she would remember it for ever. She would tell her children about it—and her grandchildren.

In the headiness of new-found love she had forgotten all about her promise to herself never to get married, never to trust the opposite sex. This was the man for her; of that she had been very sure. He would never let her down the way her father had her mother. And she had got swept along by the excitement of the occasion.

It had been the talk of the office. Love at first sight and a whirlwind affair. The other girls had been green with envy, but most of the men had been relieved because, as they'd jokingly said, they no longer needed to keep an eye on their girlfriends or wives.

'So what is it that has caused you to fade away like a wispy cloud?'

Hunter's voice broke into her thoughts, and she was grateful because she didn't want to think about what might have been. It had been a fairytale love affair, a fairytale wedding, and then *poof!* Gone! Exploded like a firework. Nothing left except memories.

'I doubt you'd be interested,' she said, deliberately keeping her chin high and her tone cool.

'Believe me, I would.' His head was bent towards her, his voice a low rumble in his throat.

His voice had urged her on so many times into the most wonderful and magical love sessions. It was deep and sexy; he had mastered the art of turning bones into jelly and blood into water. His voice had made her his prisoner. When he'd spoken to her like that she would have done anything for him.

Even now she could feel the fine threads of his web closing around her.

'I owe you nothing,' she said firmly. 'And I'd really like you to go away and leave me to enjoy myself.'

Hunter had no intention of leaving Keisha's side. When he'd seen her enter the room he had been unable to believe his eyes. Her disappearing act had been so final that he had thought never to see her again.

Three years ago he'd been captivated by her youthful innocence, by her lovely heart-shaped face and her infinitely kissable lips. He had been unable to get her out of his mind, and when she'd accepted his proposal he'd been the happiest man alive.

It hadn't occurred to him that she wasn't yet ready to be

bound by the confines of marriage. That jealousy and inse-curity would be their downfall. All he'd known was that he loved her and wanted her by his side for the rest of his life.

At his insistence Keisha had given up her job and moved into his apartment in the City. A few months later they'd moved into a beautiful house in Surrey, and he'd been happier than he'd ever been in his life. So when, just after their first wedding anniversary, Keisha had walked out on him, he'd been gutted.

He'd known she wasn't happy with the long hours he worked. Maybe it had been wrong to insist that she give up her job—but how could he have kept his attention on his work with his beautiful, sexy wife within arm's reach?

When she'd complained that she had nothing to do, when she'd declared that there were only so many times she could visit her mother or trail around the shops, he had suggested she find herself a hobby.

What he hadn't expected was for her to join a gym, and it had worried him when he overheard her on the phone to her friend Gillian, saying how sexy the men there were. And more especially when she'd mentioned one man in particu-lar. But when he'd questioned her she had declared that he was no more than a friend. That he was in fact happily married.

'Why don't you join too, then you can meet him?' she'd suggested. 'His name's Marc Collins. He's actually a friend of someone I went to school with.'

But he had declined the offer, accepting that if she was prepared for them to meet then he had nothing to worry about.

Conversely, he had known that Keisha harboured ideas that he was seeing another woman—they'd had enough ar-guments about it. But he'd thought she'd accepted that there was no one else.

How wrong he had been!

He had returned home one evening at about a quarter to midnight, after working solidly on a new advertising campaign, and she had dropped her bombshell. She had told him that she was leaving. And her eyes had been so cold and distant that he'd found it hard to believe she was the same girl who had been so passionately in love with him.

He had looked at her in total disbelief. 'Keisha, tell me you're joking.'

But she hadn't been. They'd talked long into the night and he'd used all his powers of persuasion before he had finally made her promise that she would stay. That night they'd had the best sex ever—their love life had always been amazing, but that had been something different. It had felt as though they were renewing their vows, and he'd gone to work the next day feeling ten feet tall, fully confident that they had resolved their differences.

But that evening when he'd got home she'd gone.

He'd phoned her mother. He'd phoned everyone who might know where she was. Without result. At first he'd been worried, and he'd thought about calling the police. Until he'd realised that she couldn't exactly be classed as a missing person. She'd walked out because she wasn't happy.

She had fooled him into feeling safe.

Gradually his concern had turned to anger. How could she do this to him? Why? He had thought their love was indestructible.

Then he'd found out that it had nothing to do with the long hours he kept, or her delusions about other women. She'd used that as an excuse. She was the one who'd been having an adulterous affair. She'd said that her male friend was just that—a friend, a married friend—and he'd believed her. But he'd spotted her out on the street with her arms locked around his neck—at least he'd presumed it was the same guy. Even if it wasn't, she'd clearly been infatuated with whoever it was.

She had been blatantly kissing him! In broad daylight!

Blood had fizzed in front of his eyes; he'd felt both revulsion and humiliation. She'd lied to him. His fury had known no bounds. He'd wanted to march up to her and wring her neck. And he'd wanted to knock the living daylights out of the guy embracing her. But he hadn't. What would have been the point in causing a scene when their marriage was over? He had more dignity than that.

Instead he had watched as they'd walked off, hand in hand.

It was the hardest thing he'd ever done. Hurt had sliced into his heart as fiercely as if she'd stabbed him with a knife. And with hurt had come guilt. Maybe it was his fault? Maybe if he'd spent more time with her she wouldn't have gone off with someone else? She wouldn't have felt the need for male company.

There had been so many maybes and so much heartache that his head had spun. For days he'd done nothing but blame himself, until finally he'd grown convinced that it was not all his fault. It took two to break up a marriage. Keisha was as much to blame as he was. She had lied about her platonic relationship. She had accused him of two-timing her. And yet she had been doing exactly the same thing.

He had wondered how long her affair had been going on. He'd tried to pinpoint the time their marriage had started to go downhill. It certainly hadn't been smooth going. They'd had many arguments about his long hours, and she'd become totally convinced he was seeing another woman. He'd tried to convince her that she was wrong, but clearly he'd failed.

Perhaps she'd thought that what was good enough for the goose was good enough for the gander?

Except that he'd never cheated on her. Which made her defection doubly hard to bear.

Somehow he'd picked up the pieces of his life; working harder than ever, trying to forget her, not even letting her petition for a quick divorce disturb him. And he'd thought he had succeeded.

But now, seeing her again, feeling her betrayal all over again, he knew that somehow—he didn't know how yet—he wanted to hurt her as she had hurt him. He didn't love her any more—how could he when she'd turned to another man? But he was determined that she would get her comeuppance. One way or another!

'I have no intention of going away, Keisha,' he said on a rough growl, trying to hide the anger that was building up inside him. 'As a matter of fact I'd like to dance with you.' The band had struck up and was playing a slow waltz, and without giving her time to refuse Hunter took her hand and pulled her on to the tiny square of polished floor.

At first, as fierce memories lingered, he held her more tightly than perhaps he should have done. But gradually he relaxed, and so did Keisha, and as they swayed to the music, as he deliberately talked about anything except themselves, he discovered that she wasn't entirely immune to him. Deep down inside something was still there.

Not love; he doubted now whether she ever had loved him. Probably the glamour of marrying the boss had seduced her. But there was definitely something physical happening—it had been a big part of their relationship, a massive part.

And it could work to his advantage!

* * *

Keisha was disappointed with the way her body was behaving. How could she feel anything for Hunter after all this time? It didn't make sense. When the music stopped she headed swiftly away from him.

But not fast enough. Hunter caught her hand. 'What's the hurry? The evening's only just beginning.'

'Maybe for you, but not for me,' she retorted, wrenching free. Gillian would get an earful; that was for sure. The last man in the world she had wanted to meet again was her ex husband.

Their marriage had been a huge mistake. She'd been far too young and inexperienced for the likes of Hunter. In actual fact he had been married to his work, and for light relief he'd chosen far more sophisticated women than herself. She had come a sad second best. She had wished for the moon and got only the stars. And, although she'd now discovered that she still had feelings for him, she didn't want to be caught in his trap again.

Hunter, however, was totally unmoved; he was even smiling, though she observed that it didn't quite reach his eyes. 'Tell me—who is the good lady instrumental in us meeting again?'

'It's Gillian, actually. Do you remember her?' asked Keisha. 'But I wish she'd never persuaded me to come.'

'That's a pity,' he said pleasantly. 'I'm of the opposite opinion myself.'

Keisha looked into his intense blue eyes. They were quite the most magnificent eyes she had ever seen on a man. They had been part of his attraction in the first place, long-lashed and beautifully shaped, eyes that had made her feel very special.

And still could!

Damn him!

She looked around for Gillian, but her friend was nowhere in sight.

'Are you saying that *you* are pleased to see me?' she asked, looking frowningly up at him

Hunter was tall, six feet four, while she was twelve inches shorter. She had loved the difference in their heights. Loved it when he'd picked her up and twirled her around. When he'd hugged her to him, resting his chin on her head.

'Surprised and pleased,' he answered. 'I want to know what you've been doing this last three years.' Suddenly his face darkened, and long, strong fingers gripped her upper arms. 'Exactly what you've been doing.'

Keisha felt sudden fear. This was a side of Hunter she'd not seen before. 'Let me go,' she protested. 'What are you doing? You're hurting me.'

'I'm taking you somewhere quiet,' he growled. 'Where we can talk undisturbed.'

His words were soft, but they were laced with steel, and Keisha felt a shiver of apprehension. If only Gillian were in sight she could rush over to her and insist they go home. But her friend had disappeared, and Keisha couldn't help wondering whether she had seen her with Hunter and made a tactful exit.

Gillian knew all about her divorce, of course; they had been friends for years. Gillian, however, thought Hunter was the bee's knees, and couldn't understand why Keisha would want to live without him. She had often urged her to get in touch and try to patch things up.

But Keisha had been adamant that it wouldn't work.

With her elbow held in a vice-like grip, Hunter guided her through the laughing, talking crowd to a secluded corner.

When he pushed her down onto a chair she looked mutinously into his face. 'This is a complete waste of time,' she declared.

'I don't think so.' He took a couple of glasses of champagne from a hovering waiter and pushed one across a low table towards her.

Keisha didn't want the drink, but something made her pick it up and down the whole lot in one swallow.

Hunter gave a satisfied little smile.

In three years he had matured quite dramatically. His glossy black hair, which had been almost shoulder length, was now brutally short. It showed no sign of receding, but there were a few distinguishing grey hairs at his temples.

He'd used to have twinkling eyes, but now they were serious. His thick level brows hadn't changed, but his mouth no longer smiled in that mysterious way that had churned her insides. She had used to think that he looked like a dashing highwayman. Now he was a coolly contained businessman, very much in control of himself and all those around him.

And why was she noticing all this when she didn't even want to be here? Damn! He was too much under her skin; she had never really forgotten him, especially the exciting times they'd spent together in bed. She wondered whether there was any other man in this whole world who could stir her senses so gloriously.

But marriage wasn't just about sex. A couple needed to be friends and companions as well. And most importantly of all there needed to be trust. Which was something that had been sadly lacking in their relationship.

'More champagne?'

Keisha nodded, and Hunter hailed another waiter.

'Do you like what you see?'

She instantly averted her eyes, uneasy that she had been openly studying him, but more embarrassed that he had noticed. 'You have a few grey hairs,' she announced.

'I guess it's because I've been working hard. My business has grown dramatically. I have offices in Europe now, and I'm hoping to open one in New York next year. I'm hardly ever at home.'

'Why don't I find that surprising?' she asked drily.

Hunter hissed sudden anger. 'You knew that I had no choice if I wanted to get ahead. Really, Keisha, your attitude's not changed one iota. Maybe I had a merciful release? You're not cut out to be an executive's wife.'

Keisha said nothing, picking up her glass and taking a sip of the sparkling wine. Then she twirled the crystal flute between her fingers and stared down at the tiny bubbles.

'So it's not the fact you've been missing me that's caused you to lose so much weight?' he asked, his blue eyes intent upon hers. 'It's someone else who's done this to you?'

Wouldn't it be good if she could disappear as quickly and completely as the bubbles in her glass, thought Keisha. Pop— they had gone! No more fear that they would be swallowed whole and live the rest of their lives swimming through miles of tubes—just as she was now swimming through years of revived memories.

Ignoring his question, she said, 'Actually, I'm pleased for you. You deserve success.' Yet even to her own ears she did not sound sincere.

'For that I thank you,' he acknowledged quietly, inclining his head. 'So, now that you know what I've been doing, tell me what you've been up to. Your mother told me you'd moved away.'

Keisha's eyes widened in stunned disbelief. 'You spoke to my mother?'

'What did you think?' he asked, both brows rising this time, his eyes very wide and questioning. 'That I wouldn't come looking for you?'

'She never told me.' Keisha could hardly believe that her parent had kept secret the fact that Hunter had been searching for her. And the worst part was that now she could never thank her.

'She wouldn't tell me where you were either,' he responded. 'She said that if I tried to find you I'd have her to deal with. She's a tough cookie, your mother. Lord knows what sort of tale you spun her. She spoke to me as though I were some sort of perverted idiot.'

Keisha was amazed that her mother had stood up for her like that. Not that it would have stopped Hunter if he'd been really determined. She compressed her lips and tears threatened. 'My mother died recently.'

'Oh!' he said. 'I didn't know. I'm sorry to hear that.'

And he looked it. Compassion softened his face and she had the feeling that he wanted to pull her into his arms. She hoped he wouldn't. She didn't want to experience the warmth of his body, his steady heartbeat, or the pleasure it could give her. Thinking about her mother made her vulnerable. She wished he hadn't brought the subject up.

'Don't be,' she said sharply. 'She was very ill towards the end. It was a merciful release.'

'You must miss her.'

Keisha nodded.

'So where are you living now?'

'In my mother's house,' answered Keisha reluctantly. Though for how much longer was one of the things worrying her.

'And is there a man in your life?'

It was Keisha's turn to lift a brow, and she noticed that he was watching her face closely. She hoped he wasn't thinking of suggesting she move back in with him, that they try again. Heaven help her! 'I hardly think it's any business of yours.'

His brows lifted again, but he didn't pursue the subject. Though she had a feeling she hadn't heard the last of it.

There had been no man in her life since Hunter. For the first twelve months she had been too fragile, and since then she had nursed her sick mother and had had no time for boy-friends.

And she didn't want any more of these personal questions.

'I'm getting out of here,' she declared, scrambling to her feet. 'I'll call a taxi. If you see Gillian tell her I've gone.'

But Hunter stopped her. 'If you insist on going then I will take you myself,' he said, in that deep, sexy voice that impinged on her nerve-ends every time she heard it. It was low and persuasive at this moment, snaring her, and when he caught her wrist and held on to it while he too rose from his chair Keisha knew she was lost.

He had a stranglehold on both her body and her senses.

There was no escape.

CHAPTER TWO

HUNTER'S CAR WAS black and sleek and luxurious. It smelled of leather and his cologne, and as Keisha sank into the seat beside him she marvelled at how far he had come in the last few years.

And she could have been a part of it if she hadn't left him.

The thought gave her no pleasure. He might have all the trappings of wealth, perhaps even more money than he knew what to do with, but was he truly happy? 'Have *you* married again?' she asked bluntly. There was no ring on his finger either, and there'd been no beauty hanging on to his arm. Surely there would have been if he'd got either a wife or a girl-friend?

'I've had no time,' he answered, slanting a tight, smiling glance in her direction.

'You're married to money—is that it?' she enquired, keeping her voice honey sweet and her eyes on the road in front of them. It annoyed her that simply by looking at him he disturbed her senses.

He was one of that band of men who could turn a woman's head without even trying. He had certainly turned hers— quite magnificently! She had thought herself the luckiest girl in the world when he'd asked her to marry him.

'Money isn't my slave, if that's what you're suggesting,' he answered smoothly. 'I enjoy being successful, I admit that, and I enjoy being able to go anywhere or do anything, but it isn't the be all and end all of my life.'

'So why haven't you remarried?' she asked, turning to look at him as his lips gave a rueful smile. 'It can't be because there's a shortage of women in your life.'

'Of course not,' he answered smoothly. 'I could have my pick of maybe a dozen girls at any one time—it comes with the territory.' He shot her a sharply dangerous glance. 'But it's not worth it. I learned my lesson many years ago.'

'Are you suggesting that I flung myself at you?' Keisha's tone was indignant. If anyone had done the pursuing it had been Hunter. Not that she hadn't enjoyed the chase!

'You're saying that you didn't drop that file deliberately?' he asked. 'Come on, Keisha, it's the oldest trick in the book. Of course I didn't realise it at the time, but...' He gave a tiny shrug and let his words fade into thin air.

'Would I have walked out on you if I'd married you for your money?' Keisha asked with a questioning stare. 'I don't think so, Hunter. You're talking rubbish.'

It was a relief when they pulled up outside her house. It was a two-up-and-two-down terraced property, very modest but very comfortable, and her mother had loved it.

'Thank you for the lift,' she said, opening the door and scrambling out almost before he had stopped the car. 'You won't forget to tell Gillian that I've come home?'

'I'm sure she carries her mobile, you'd best call her yourself,' he said drily, sliding out the other side and following her up the short path.

'You don't have to see me in,' declared Keisha in panic. This was the very last thing she wanted. She had left the party to get away from Hunter, not have him pressing further attentions on her.

'A gentleman would never allow a lady to enter an empty house alone.'

Keisha put her key in the lock and opened the door a few inches, but before she could tell him that she was safe and he could go his hand reached over her shoulder and pushed the door wider. With his other hand in the small of her back, he urged her inside.

'There is absolutely no need for this,' she insisted, tossing her head in desperation. 'As you can see, all's well. You can go back to your party.'

But Hunter had other ideas. His smile was cruel. 'We're long overdue a serious conversation. Have you any idea how I felt when you walked out on me?'

'I don't want to talk to you.' Keisha flashed desperate green eyes. 'You and I have nothing further to say to each other. I thank you for the lift, but now I want you to go.'

'Are you going to make me?' He folded his arms across his broad chest and dared her to challenge him. He was all male, strong and indomitable, and Keisha knew that she was fighting a losing battle.

She heaved a sigh of despair. 'You're wasting your time. You know the reason I left. We can do nothing but go over old ground.'

'Then it's old ground we go over,' he answered simply.

There was no entrance hall at the property. The door led straight into a living room filled with old but much loved furniture. It was small, but felt even smaller with Hunter inside. 'Please, sit down,' she said faintly. 'I'll make us some coffee.'

She needed breathing space. He filled it with his presence, leaving her nowhere to hide.

Hunter needed no second bidding. Off came his dinner jacket and bow tie, and the top three buttons of his shirt were undone before he relaxed into an old leather chair.

Keisha gave an inward groan. She hadn't meant to give him an invitation to make himself comfortable. The matter was getting out of hand; he looked as though he was ready to stay for hours.

She gritted her teeth and fled the room.

When she returned Hunter's head had dropped back and his eyes were closed. Heaven forbid that he was asleep, she thought. From experience she knew that he was a heavy sleeper; there would be no getting rid of him. He would be here the whole night!

But as she put the cups down on a side table Hunter opened heavy eyelids. His slow smile was predatory, and uneasiness sent a chill down her spine. He had something in mind and she had no idea what.

She perched on the edge of a chair, as far away from him as she could get in this tiny room, and waited.

'You look as though you're afraid of me,' he said. 'Why is that, I wonder?'

'Because you wouldn't be here if you didn't have some ulterior motive.'

An eyebrow rose. 'Don't you think you're being fanciful?' And he paused before adding, 'As I said before, I'm merely being a gentleman.'

Keisha's lips twisted into a disbelieving smile. 'Seeing me home was gentlemanly, but making yourself comfortable is not. You're not welcome here, Hunter.'

'As you've made very clear,' he acknowledged. 'But surely a little conversation over a cup of coffee is nothing to worry about?'

It was when the man was Hunter Donahue!

'Why are you showing such an interest in me after all this time?' she asked, picking up her cup and saucer and holding on to them as though they were a lifeline. She needed a barrier between them—a brick wall would have been preferable! He was unnerving her with his intense blue eyes and thoughtful stare.

'I didn't expect you to walk out on me—not after our conversation,' he said. 'It wasn't a very adult thing to do, was it? Unless, of course, there was some other reason that you left?' His voice sharpened, became crisp and suspicious. 'Something—or maybe someone—you didn't tell me about?'

'I simply couldn't put up with your lifestyle,' she flared. Had he no idea how abandoned she'd felt? Or how hurt she'd been? Or how foolish she'd felt for agreeing to marry him in the first place when he was so far out of her league? Her emotions had been all over the place—and he'd simply never seen it.

'I saw more of our neighbour than I did you,' she added defensively. 'Maybe if you'd let me carry on working it wouldn't have been so bad, but—'

'Which neighbour?' he cut in sharply.

'Oh, for heaven's sake!' exclaimed Keisha. 'What's that got to do with it? Mrs Smith—she used to pop round for a cup of tea now and then. Sometimes I'd take her shopping. She was very bad on her feet. But you wouldn't know that, would you?' she asked sarcastically. 'You were never home long enough to get to know your neighbours.'

'OK, enough about this Mrs Smith,' he said. 'I'm more interested in where you ran away to. Your mother was very protective of your privacy.'

'What did you expect?' asked Keisha. 'Actually, I'm surprised you had time to search for me.'

His brows drew into a harsh frown. 'You really believe I thought so little of you—and our marriage?'

Keisha shrugged. 'It's the impression you gave.'

'You didn't think it strange that I didn't try to find you?'

'I did, yes,' she admitted. 'But it simply confirmed my belief that you put your work first. Or that maybe you were relieved I'd given you the freedom to carry on your affairs?'

Hunter hissed his anger, and he was silent for several long seconds, fighting his inner tension. Finally he sighed. 'It just goes to prove that you never really knew me. Where did you go?'

'Scotland,' she admitted quietly and reluctantly. 'I rented a cottage and found myself a job.'

There must have been something in her voice, because Hunter frowned, his brows drawing together in total incredulity. 'Scotland? About as far away as you could go without leaving the country. What did your mother think about you living so far away?'

'We were in touch daily.'

'But you didn't come back down to see her?' His tone was growing more and more disbelieving. And his voice was getting louder and louder.

'I did occasionally,' she admitted. 'Naturally I'd have much rather she came to me, but she wasn't in—'

'You were afraid of bumping into me?' he interrupted abrasively.

Keisha didn't have to answer; it was there in her eyes.

'Do you still hate me, Keisha?'

'I've never hated you, Hunter,' she answered, quietly and truthfully. 'I simply wasn't happy in our marriage. I wanted more from life.'

'But you don't love me either?' His voice was equally low, and his eyes never left hers.

Keisha shook her head, at the same time shaking off the sensation of closeness that had suddenly overwhelmed her. 'No!' She shifted uneasily. Because, although she didn't love him, she still found him devastatingly sexy. He still managed to arouse feelings inside her body that she would rather were not there.

A tiny smile played about Hunter's generous lips.

Heaven help her if he ever found out the truth, Keisha thought to herself! One inch of encouragement and he would have her in his bed again before she could even think about it.

'So what sort of work did you do in Scotland?'

Keisha was relieved that he'd changed the subject. Their conversation had been getting far too intimate for her liking.

'I worked in an advertising office.'

Hunter's brows rose. 'Perhaps I know them?'

'I wouldn't think so,' she said. 'They were very small.'

'Were you happy there?'

Keisha nodded.

'And you had a boyfriend to keep you company?'

She let her breath out noisily. 'Why do you keep asking? Of what interest is it to you?'

Hunter lifted his shoulders in a lazy shrug, his lips twisting at the corners. 'Perhaps I just want to find out whether he—they—matched up to me?' But although he gave the impression of being relaxed there was a tautness about him that Keisha could not help but notice.

He didn't like to think that she'd been with any other man.

'Such conceit!' she tossed scornfully.

And nor did she want to think about the good times they'd had. No one could ever match up to him; that was a fact. 'How about you?' she asked, turning the tables. 'How many girl-friends have you had?'

Dark brows rose. 'Why should I have had any when the only girl I've ever truly loved walked out on me?'

Keisha's head jerked. 'Don't try to fool me. There have always been other women in your life.'

Blue eyes met green. 'I'm very serious. You've no idea, Keisha, how much you hurt me. When you filed for divorce I couldn't believe it. I thought that when you'd had time to think things over you'd come back to me.'

'Then you are either very stupid or very naïve,' she declared strongly. 'And *I* must be incredibly stupid to be sitting here having this conversation with you. It's a complete waste of time.'

'I'd like to take you out.'

Keisha closed her eyes briefly. There was one part of her, very deep down inside, that wanted to say yes. The part she had thought was dead and now found was very much alive. But the sane part of her mind knew what a mistake it would be.

Hunter had a massive ego if he really thought she would agree. 'You're unreal,' she said.

'Am I?' he asked, his mouth curving into a smile. 'Touch me. You'll soon find out how real I am.'

'You know what I'm talking about.'

'No, I don't. Tell me.' He spread his hands expansively. 'We have the whole evening.'

Keisha felt as though she would die from asphyxiation if he didn't go soon. He was taking all the air from the room, filling it with a black fear that was totally inexplicable. Unless it was the feelings he was still able to invoke inside her that she was afraid of.

It was not a thought she found any pleasure in. In fact it

both alarmed and horrified her. 'No, we don't have the whole evening,' she said, quietly but firmly. 'I want you to drink your coffee and go.' She picked up her cup and took a swallow before realising that it was still too hot.

Gallantly, though, she did not show it. She waited for him to follow suit, and willed him to scald his throat. She wanted him to suffer as she had suffered. He still seemed to have no idea how much he had hurt her.

Although maybe—and it was just a little maybe—she was the one at fault. The simple truth was that she really hadn't been mature enough for marriage. She'd had an idealistic dream of time spent together, of long, exciting love sessions, of making babies, and Hunter always at her side. When it hadn't turned out like that, when he'd spent more time working than he had with her, when he'd come home smelling of someone else's perfume, she'd known their marriage was over and had run like a scared cat.

Not only that, though, she'd had visions of her mother's unhappy marriage—of a husband who neglected her, who was absent far more often than he was at home. Maybe for different reasons than Hunter's, but even so it would almost have been like history repeating itself. It had ruined her mother's health, and Keisha had been afraid that her own sanity would be at risk if she continued in her marriage any longer.

Hunter took one sip of his coffee and then put the cup back down. 'Maybe I will go. Maybe tomorrow would be a better time to talk—when you're in a more receptive frame of mind. I'll pick you up at ten.'

And with that sweeping statement, before she could even say a word, he grabbed his jacket and walked out of the house.

Keisha was left feeling utterly inadequate. Why hadn't she spoken? Why hadn't she told him that she never wanted to see him again? Now she would be compelled to face him in the morning—and what was the betting that he wouldn't take no for an answer a second time?

Sleep evaded her that night. Instead her mind went back to her first date with Hunter…

At twenty-nine, Hunter Donahue had been much older and far more sophisticated than Keisha, and when he'd turned up at her house looking suave and elegant, in dark trousers and a white shirt, she had felt sudden panic.

'Wh-where are we going?' she asked huskily as he escorted her out to his car.

'The world's our oyster. Where would you like to go?'

'I don't know,' she whispered. 'I'll leave it up to you.' Heavens, she was so nervous.

Hunter smiled, a lovely warm smile that began to melt the fear in her heart. 'I know a nice quiet little restaurant by the river. Would that suit?'

Keisha nodded.

It was the beginning of a whirlwind affair. His kisses were to die for and his lovemaking out of this world. And when he proposed to her after they'd been going out for only a few weeks she could hardly believe it.

'Are you serious?' she asked. She wanted to say yes, she wanted to shout it from the rooftops, but she had to be sure first. This was a tremendous step.

'Extremely serious,' he answered, and his eyes told her that it was true. They were the most intense blue she had ever seen them, and he looked at her with so much love that she felt she would die.

Their wedding was a fairytale dream, and their honeymoon in Madeira out of this world, but what she hadn't realised was that Hunter was obsessed with making money, and over the following months he spent so many hours at his office that she hardly saw him.

She felt distinctly lonely and neglected. She tried to keep herself busy, but there was a limit to what she could do, and even going to the gym didn't help. She began to wonder whether he had tired of her, whether it was an affair that was keeping him away. He was sometimes too exhausted to make love, which was such a change from the rampant male he'd been in the early weeks of their marriage that there had to be something different happening in his life.

And when one night he returned home and she smelled another woman's perfume on him her heart fell with a thud into the pit of her stomach.

'Have you been with another woman?' she asked fiercely, pulling away from his kiss and staring into the blueness of his eyes.

'God, no!' he exclaimed at once. 'As if I'd do that.'

'I can smell perfume on you.'

'Maybe,' he acknowledged with a shrug. 'I've been entertaining a female client.'

'And you got so close that her perfume is lingering on your clothes?'

Hunter pursed his lips wryly. 'Actually, she—'

But Keisha didn't want to listen to excuses. 'Did you take her to bed?' she asked swiftly.

Hunter stiffened, his blue eyes suddenly fierce and condemning. 'Are you questioning my integrity? Don't you love me enough to trust me?'

'Of course I love you,' she replied, noticing that he hadn't actually answered her question. 'The trouble is I love you too much. I miss you.' It was a plea from her heart. 'I want you, Hunter, so badly. I don't want any other woman to have you.'

'And none shall,' he declared gruffly, folding her in his arms and kissing her soundly. That night his lovemaking was better than ever. And when he began to keep more reasonable hours Keisha knew that she had been mistaken.

But after a few weeks the late nights started all over again, and her insecurity grew to such an extent that she couldn't help tackling him. 'Who is it this time that's keeping you away from me?' she demanded to know. She had waited up for him and began her attack the moment he entered the house. 'The same woman or someone else?'

Hunter frowned harshly. 'Keisha, I will not allow these ridiculous accusations. What the hell's the matter with you? Have I ever given you reason to think that I'm having an affair?'

'Yes—you had perfume on you,' she riposted quickly.

'And do I have a woman's perfume on me now?' he asked, pulling her close. 'Go on, smell me! Do I?'

Keisha had to confess that he didn't. 'I can't think of any other reason why you keep such ridiculous hours if it's not a woman,' she retorted. 'It's not as though you need the money. Your company's doing very well.'

'And why is it doing well?' he asked fiercely. 'Because I put in all the hours God gives to make it that way. It's my driving force—haven't you realised that yet? And while we're on the subject of infidelity, perhaps I should be the one questioning you?'

Keisha head jerked and she frowned. What was he talking about?

'Do you realise how often you mention Marc Collins these days?'

'Do I?' she asked. She wasn't aware of it.

'Yes, you do,' he answered, his voice abrasive, his eyes accusing. 'And you seem to be going to the gym far more frequently. Maybe I'm the one who has reason to be suspicious?'

Keisha laughed. 'Really, Hunter, he's just a friend. I told you that. Don't you believe that a woman can have a male friend?' Hunter was never around long enough for her to have a decent conversation. She needed someone to talk to, and Marc was always willing to lend an ear.

'Not a woman as sexy as you,' he growled, and he pulled her into his arms and kissed her. Hot, passionate kisses, punishing kisses. And soon Marc was forgotten. Everything was forgotten—except the heady excitement of exploring each other's bodies.

Somehow they seesawed their way through marriage for almost twelve months. There were times when everything went along smoothly and she was the happiest woman alive, and others when her uncertainties reared their ugly heads and they had unholy rows.

Finally Keisha was forced to accept that enough was enough. She couldn't punish herself any longer.

CHAPTER THREE

'I'M LEAVING YOU, Hunter.'

A frown sliced into Hunter's brow, so deep that it might have been cut by a razor, and he stared at her in total disbelief. 'Keisha, tell me you're joking.'

'I'm deadly serious,' she said quietly.

'But why?' He looked genuinely surprised.

'Do I have to spell it out?' she asked impatiently. 'Isn't it obvious? The rows we've been having, the hours you keep. I can't put up with it any longer. I want a husband who cares.'

It was partly her own fault, she realised that. She ought never to have married so young, and especially not to a man who thought more of his work than he did her. But that didn't alter the fact that she was dreadfully unhappy.

'Keisha, of course I care about you.' He tried to take her into his arms but she pushed him away. 'I love you deeply,' he told her, his expression confirming his words. 'You're the best part of my life.'

Her eyes flared a brilliant green. 'Then it's a pity you haven't thought about that before. Because I don't want to be married to you any longer. My bags are already packed. I'm leaving first thing in the morning.'

'You can't do this.' Hunter's voice rose, loud and angry.

'Believe me, I can,' she retorted.

'I won't let you.' He stood tall and proud, looking down at her with eyes full of fury. 'You married me for better or for worse.'

'Then I was a fool,' she snapped. 'Because I didn't realise how bad the worse would be. I can't take any more.'

His jaw tightened and his eyes became frighteningly black. But Keisha refused to back down. If she did so now she would be condemning herself to a lifetime of hell. She ought not to have told him that she was going; she ought to have just left.

Had she been subconsciously wondering whether he would persuade her to stay? Whether he would promise to change his habits? If so she was a fool, because Hunter would never change—not in a hundred years.

'I love you, Keisha.'

He said it so calmly that it was scary.

'And if you'd stop being angry for a moment you'd admit that you need me.'

If he thought that much of her he wouldn't neglect her, thought Keisha. She wanted to be out enjoying life with him. She'd just turned twenty for goodness' sake; she couldn't handle these long nights in alone. The days were bad enough, but the evenings as well...

'Yes, I do need you,' she answered sadly. 'That's the whole point. I need you but I haven't got you.'

They talked long into the night, and when they finally went to bed Hunter pulled her into his arms and made sure that she felt safe and cherished. Hunter in this mood she wouldn't dream of leaving, but she knew that his promises never lasted.

The next morning he made her swear that she'd still be there when he got back, but Keisha had no intention of keeping her promise. As soon as he'd gone she slung her bags into her car and left the house for good.

Keisha's retrospective thoughts had kept her awake for most of the night; nevertheless she was ready when Hunter came to pick her up the next morning. Not that she welcomed the prospect of spending time with him. If she'd known where to contact him she would have phoned and cancelled their date.

If it could be called a date!

He had coerced her into it. As far as she was concerned they had nothing to say to each other. The past was just that—past. There was no point bringing it up, discussing what might have been. It was over, done with. They were divorced. Why did he want to see her again?

He arrived at ten on the dot, devastatingly handsome in grey trousers and a white silk shirt. Despite her misgivings, Keisha's heart skipped a beat.

She had dressed down deliberately, in a pair of white trousers and a cerise top, and she didn't expect Hunter to pass any comment.

But he did.

'You look good,' he said. 'Not at all as though you've spent a sleepless night wondering how you can get out of seeing me.'

Keisha frowned. How did he know that she'd lain awake? Unless, of course, he had done exactly the same. She looked carefully for shadows beneath his eyes but there none. He was the same as always. Gorgeously sexy!

There ought to be a law forbidding men to look like he did. It should never be allowed. His face was strong, with a square jaw and beautifully moulded lips. She only had to look at them to want to feel his kisses.

She gave her head a mental shake, trying to squash both her thoughts and her traitorous feelings. 'If you had an ounce of decency you would have cancelled,' she told him coolly. 'In fact I don't know why you asked me out in the first place. Talking won't help. We're two different people now, each with our own lives. We have nothing in common.'

'I beg to differ.' A wide smile stretched those kissable lips, revealing equally beautiful white teeth. Was there nothing about this man that was not perfect? Keisha asked herself.

'We have a marriage in common.'

Keisha looked sceptically into his eyes. 'Was it ever a real marriage?' And, with a complete change of subject, 'Where are we going?'

'I thought maybe a picnic somewhere.'

Keisha looked at his smart linen trousers and expensive white shirt. 'A picnic?' she asked, her tone incredulous, her fine brows rising.

'Have you any better suggestions?'

She could tell him to get lost. Would that do any good? She doubted it. 'None,' she answered abruptly.

'One thing we do need is privacy,' he said. 'And since you don't seem to think much of my suggestion I think maybe I'll take you back to my house. We can picnic on my lawn, if you like,' he added with a whimsical smile. 'Or maybe we'll be a bit more sophisticated and go out for lunch—after we've talked.'

Keisha knew she had no choice. She ought not to have opened the door to him. Or, better still, she ought to have gone out and let him fume on her doorstep. It was a ridiculous situation.

'Or we can talk here, and then I can throw you out when I've had enough,' she declared, her lips tight, her green eyes revealing inner tension. Which was enough to make her feel like an over-tight guitar string that might snap at any moment.

'No!' he declared firmly. 'We need space.'

'In case I throw something at you?'

Hunter smiled. 'Maybe.'

And so he drove her to his house on the outskirts of the City. It wasn't like the one they'd bought in Surrey when they'd got married. It was a mansion in all but name. Keisha's eyes widened when she saw it. 'You've certainly gone up in the world,' she said.

It had a security gate at the end of the drive, and looked like something out of a period movie. As they drove up to the house she saw lawns leading down to the Thames, and a boat moored to a wide wooden deck.

'Like I said, my business is doing very well for itself,' he said. 'It's far exceeded my dreams.'

'And I suppose you're still putting in those ludicrous hours?' she challenged. 'Why do you need a house this size if there's only you living here?' What she was really asking was whether there was another woman in his life.

'Because I entertain a lot,' he answered. 'I hold corporate meetings here—business weekends, in fact. It works better than booking conference rooms. I have loyal staff who do all the organising and look after my every need.'

Keisha's brows rose. This was money talking. Real money. And here was she without a penny to call her own. Was she sorry that she was not a part of it? Or glad? Would she have enjoyed all these trappings of wealth? Who knew what might have happened if she hadn't run out on him?

Hunter had also lain awake for a good deal of last night. He'd been flabbergasted when he saw Keisha. Considering that she had disappeared without trace, it had been like seeing an apparition. She was still beautiful, despite how thin she was, and regardless of the way she'd treated him he couldn't help thinking how much he'd lost.

He'd thought their marriage was perfect, and had found it hard to believe that she'd wanted to leave him. When he had discovered that blaming his hard work had been nothing more than a smokescreen, when he'd seen her with her arms around another man, all hell had broken loose inside him.

And now that they'd met again he'd spent all night working out how to get his revenge. It was a simple plan, really. He would make her fall in love with him again and then he would dump her—just as callously as she had dumped him. She would experience hurt and pain and bewilderment; she would rack her brains to find out where she had failed him.

It would destroy her.

While he would feel nothing except triumph.

But first would be the very pleasurable experience of gaining her trust again. He might hate her for walking out on him, for cheating on him, for making him look like a fool, but he still ached for her sexy little body. And he fully intended to take advantage of it!

Hunter watched her face as he showed her over his house. He was proud of his achievement, and Keisha's expression was stunned to say the least. Was she regretting walking away from all that he could have given her?

It was hard to believe that she was still living in the same tiny cottage that she'd been brought up in. He was naturally sorry to hear that her mother had died, but surely Keisha could have done better for herself? To still live in that cramped little house didn't make sense.

'What do you think?' he asked as they finished their inside tour and began walking down towards the river.

'It's magnificent,' she said.

'And it could all have been yours,' he responded, quietly awaiting her reaction.

Not that Keisha had ever wished for the moon. Indeed, she'd been shocked when he had asked her out on their first date. He had almost expected her to say, *Who? Me?* and look round to see if there was anyone behind her.

He had discovered that she worked mainly to support her mother, and although he still found it hard to understand why she had run away from him, he had found it inconceivable to believe she had left her mother in the lurch too.

Perhaps she'd been sending money to her parent? Salving her conscience that way? Whatever the situation, he'd not been able to find out about it. Keisha's mother had kept admirably quiet about her daughter's whereabouts. For that he respected her, even though it had angered him at the time when she'd stonewalled every enquiry he made.

Keisha must have cast him as the biggest villain out.

And now she was going to get her just deserts.

'I'm waiting for your answer,' he said.

Keisha frowned. 'Did you ask me something?'

'I said all this could have been yours. Do you have any regrets?' He watched her face closely. It hadn't changed much. With her green eyes and dimples and her smooth skin it still held the innocence that had first attracted him.

She shook her head vehemently. 'None at all! I'm not materialistic—you should know that.'

'So you prefer living in your mother's old house?'

'I have little choice.'

He frowned. 'What do you mean?'

'I mean I can't afford to move.'

Hunter looked at her closely, and for the first time saw the pain deep behind her eyes. He took her arm and led her to the rose arbour. 'I think we need to talk.'

Keisha looked as though she didn't want to, but he was determined to find out what had happened to make her so vulnerable. He felt fairly certain that it had nothing to do with her walking out on him.

Had the boyfriend something to do with it? Had he left her in the lurch? Anger filled him. This was the woman he had once loved; he would never have hurt her. Never! And to think that someone else had made his blood boil!

'So why can't you afford it?' It was hard keeping his voice quiet and even, but he knew that if he wanted her to talk then he would have to. 'What are you doing these days?'

Keisha shrugged. 'Temporary work.'

'Why haven't you got a permanent job?' he queried.

'Because,' she said, so softly that he assumed she didn't really want him to hear, 'I was out of work for a long time looking after my mother, and now it seems no one wants to employ me.'

'Really?' Far from feeling sorry for her he felt pleased. In fact he felt jubilant. Fate was on his side. She was playing right into his hands. This could work very well to his advantage. 'Maybe I can help?'

Keisha looked at him warily. 'I want nothing from you.'

'Can you afford to turn me down?' he asked, keeping his voice low and sympathetic.

He saw her brace herself; he saw her struggling with emotion. 'I couldn't work for you. Not again.'

Hunter allowed himself a small smile. 'Maybe you need time to think it over?'

Keisha closed her eyes. What she ought to do was snap his hand off. She needed a good, solid job—desperately! She would be a fool not to take him up on his offer. But working for Hunter again? How soul destroying would that be?

Except that maybe she wouldn't see much of him. He was the top man; he was very busy; he would be here, there and everywhere. Perhaps even abroad a lot of the time? She would have nothing to worry about.

She was very much aware of the clean, fresh masculine smell of him, so close to her nostrils that it was like breathing him in, filling herself with his sexy male body, allowing memories to come flooding back.

One memory in particular.

It had been their honeymoon night. They had showered after their flight, and then sat on their hotel balcony watching the incessant movement of the ocean, watching a blood-red sun slowly sink, marvelling at the drama taking place in the sky.

Their balcony hadn't been overlooked, and both of them had been as naked as the day they were born. Hunter had warned her on the flight over that this was the way he intended to keep her for the whole seven days.

An army of butterflies had filled Keisha's stomach at the prospect, but her inhibitions had flown once they were there, and there on their balcony the scent of Hunter had drugged her. She'd no longer wanted to watch the sea or the sky; she'd wanted to make love!

She'd drunk in the essence of him, inhaled it deep into her soul, and then she had taken him by the hand and led him through to their bedroom. What had happened afterwards had been out of this world. There on that magical island, on that first night of the rest of their life together, they had reached heights never dreamed of—and she had thought if that was what their future was going to be like then she was one hell of a happy woman.

But of course it hadn't ended up like that, and drinking him in now, smelling that same pagan smell, feeling sensations desperately trying to make themselves known all over again, created an irrational fear.

Fear *and* need!

Foolish desire!

Having anything to do with Hunter was a disaster waiting to happen.

And yet she needed a job. He was her only hope! He was offering her a lifeline. It would be stupid to throw it back in his face because of something that had happened three years ago.

'Have you thought about it?'

'What would I be doing?' she asked next.

Hunter gave her a devilish smile. 'My PA is about to go on maternity leave. I've not yet found a replacement. You'll do very nicely.'

Keisha was horrified. She couldn't! She wouldn't! She wanted distance between them, not togetherness.

'You look shocked!'

'I am. I can't work that closely with you.'

'Why ever not?' he asked pleasantly, though she feared his pleasantness was that of a wolf about to pounce.

'Because—because…' Her voice tailed off miserably. She could come up with no convincing justification.

'There, you see—you have no excuse.' Hunter's lips curled upwards in a gleeful smile. 'The matter's settled.'

'No, it isn't,' declared Keisha bravely. 'I need time to think about it. I hadn't envisaged working so closely with you. I'll think about it overnight and give you my decision in the morning.'

Hunter's smile was slow and confident. 'And we both know what it will be.'

Keisha shook her head. 'No, we don't. Maybe I do need a job, but I'm not that desperate.'

Mocking brows lifted. 'Brave words, my beautiful Keisha! If what you've told me is true, then you'd be a fool to turn me down.'

She didn't think so. She would be a fool to line herself up for more heartache—because surely that was what would happen? Spending time together would be disastrous.

'You think what you like,' she tossed irritably. 'I'd like to go home now.'

'But you've only just got here,' he declared with a fierce frown.

'I made a mistake. And if you don't want to take me I'll ring for a taxi.'

'And spend money you can ill afford?' he queried irritably. 'If you're that determined I'll take you.'

But he wasn't pleased, and he drove her home in grim-faced silence.

Keisha was relieved that he wasn't speaking, because she had nothing to say to him. Her thoughts were too full. His job offer was more than generous, given their circumstances, and the practical half of her knew that she ought to jump at it. But the sane half, the half that was afraid of what might happen between them, told her she would be a fool to even think of accepting.

He drew up outside her house and finally spoke. 'I can't keep my offer open. I need someone straight away.' He was in business mode now, serious and brusque. 'Ring me first thing tomorrow or forget it.'

Keisha shot out of the car. 'I'll forget it.' And she slammed the door.

So that was that, she thought as she let herself in. She'd turned down the only decent job offer she was likely to get. Was she stupid or what?

When she found a hand delivered envelope on her mat and read what was inside, Keisha realised that she had been very stupid indeed.

CHAPTER FOUR

KEISHA'S LANDLORD HAD finally lost patience. He was giving her twenty-four hours to pay what she owed him—or be evicted.

Keisha sat down heavily, staring at the piece of paper. She was in so much debt that she wasn't altogether surprised, though she had hoped he would wait a bit longer—until she had found a permanent job that would pay her enough.

None had been in the offing. Until today.

Until she had foolishly thrown the offer back in Hunter's face.

How long she sat holding the threatening letter Keisha didn't know. What she did know was that there was only one option open to her. But the very thought of phoning Hunter and grovelling was abhorrent.

It took her all day to make that phone call. In fact it was almost bedtime, and even then she very nearly put the receiver down before he had time to answer. Perhaps he wouldn't be in. Perhaps she was wasting her time. It could be that he wouldn't want her now. All sorts of excuses sprang into her mind.

And then she heard his voice.

Deep and sexy! Enough to curl her toes! Enough to warn her of the danger she could be in.

'It's me.' Her voice was squeaky-quiet, but he heard and recognised it.

'Keisha?' She knew he was smiling. 'You've changed your mind?'

'Yes,' she whispered.

'I'm glad you've seen sense. We start work at eight thirty. Do you have a car or shall I pick you up?'

Keisha grimaced. 'I could take the bus if you tell me—'

'Nonsense!' he cut in sharply. 'I'll pick you up at eight. Be ready.'

'There's something more,' she whispered miserably, glad she didn't have to do this to his face. How mortifying would that be? 'I need—could I—I mean, would it be possible to—?' Oh, hell, how could she ask such a thing?

'Spit it out, Keisha.'

She sensed he was losing patience.

'My rent's overdue.'

A second's silence… And then, 'So you need an advance? Is that what you're saying?'

She nodded miserably even though he couldn't see, wincing as she managed a faint, 'Yes.'

'Is your landlord making demands?'

'Yes.'

'Why didn't you tell me earlier?'

'There was a note waiting for me.'

'I'll be right over.'

'No, don't. It—' But already the line had gone dead.

Keisha cursed silently to herself. The last thing she wanted was a face-to-face discussion about her financial affairs. How embarrassing would it be?

She paced her living room as she waited for Hunter. Her heart thumped loud enough to be heard down the street, and she twisted her hands fitfully together. This was going to be worse even than when she had threatened to walk out on him. Worse in a different way. This was begging. Something she had never done before.

When she heard his car draw up she opened the door, then moved back into the room. When Hunter entered she was perched on the edge of a chair, still wringing her hands nervously together.

'I'm sorry. I didn't mean you to—'

But again he cut her short. 'How much are you in debt?'

When she told him he whistled through his teeth.

'What's been going on?'

'It cost me a lot when my mother was ill. I wanted the best care for her. I've managed to pay off the private medical bills, but my rent's been mounting up and—well—I'm afraid what I earn barely covers my needs.'

'So why didn't you tell me all this? Why didn't you come to me earlier?' Hunter looked at her as though she were a complete idiot.

Keisha shook her head. 'How could I ask my ex for money? It would have been far too demeaning. And I wouldn't be asking you now if you hadn't promised me a job. Except that it looks like it's too late,' she added with a deep sigh. 'I'll be homeless tomorrow,' Keisha finished, handing Hunter the note.

'So it would appear,' announced Hunter grimly. 'I think the best thing would be for you to move in with me. You can't be happy living here any more.'

'Oh, but I am,' insisted Keisha, horrified by the thought. 'I love this house. I've spent most of my life here. I have happy memories.'

'But you can take your memories with you,' he reasoned. 'This is nothing more than bricks and mortar. It's not a home any more; it's just a house. You'd be far better off out of here.'

Keisha was adamant. She ignored the pressure he was putting on her, the intentness in his cobalt eyes. Living with Hunter would be like living with the devil. 'I don't happen to think so. We have a past, Hunter. And not a happy one. I want to stay here.'

He lifted his shoulders. 'So be it. But I think you're making a big mistake. The offer will be there if you should ever change your mind.'

'I won't,' she retorted quickly.

'Give me your bill. I'll see to it first thing tomorrow.'

Silently Keisha handed the piece of paper to him.

He tucked it into his pocket and stood up. 'Eight in the morning, then?'

She nodded. 'And thank you, Hunter. I really do appreciate it.'

'Maybe a kiss would be better than words?'

Keisha winced inside. A kiss would arouse feelings she didn't want to acknowledge. Yet under the circumstances how could she refuse? She owed him now. The last thing she had wanted was to be beholden to this man but she was—at least until she had paid back her debt.

She stood on tiptoe and pecked him on the cheek. 'Thank you, Hunter.' But before she could move his arms came round her and his mouth found hers, and the light kiss she had intended turned into something more.

It was a deliberate assault on her senses, almost a declaration that because she was in his debt he could do what he liked. The hell he could! Keisha jerked away and fury flashed from her brilliant green eyes. 'That sort of kiss I can do without.'

Hunter's lips quirked. 'What a pity! I was rather enjoying it.'

Keisha wanted to say more, but knew she didn't dare if she wanted the job. How foolish would it be to lose it before she had even started? Hunter had got her where he wanted and she'd best not forget it.

But kissing was well out of the question. She would do her job to the best of her ability; other than that she would have nothing to do with him. Thank goodness she had stood firm about keeping her house. Or goodness knew what might have happened next. Kissing could lead to…

She didn't dare let her thoughts go any further.

'I'll be leaving, then.' He turned towards the door and Keisha's relief knew no bounds. She was grateful to him, of course she was, but she wanted to be rid of him.

She wanted room to breathe.

And it was not until the door closed behind him that she was able to do precisely that. She took in great gulping breaths and then asked herself why she was being so foolish.

She had nothing to fear from Hunter. She was a capable woman now, not an infatuated teenager. If she didn't want him to kiss her all she had to do was tell him. It was as simple as that.

But Keisha had found that nothing was simple in this life. Her marriage hadn't been trouble-free. Running away to Scotland hadn't been easy. Looking after her mother hadn't been without complications. And most definitely working for Hunter would not be straightforward.

She locked the door, turned off all the lights, and went up to bed.

But all she could think about was spending time with Hunter tomorrow. Working for him, with him, doing everything a personal assistant did. Not that she'd ever been one before, but she knew what it involved. She would be virtually his right-hand woman. As well as business arrangements she would be ordering flowers for his girlfriend—or maybe girlfriends. There could be many. Booking hotels and restaurants and so on.

She would learn every intimate detail of his life!

When she finally dropped off, her sleep was disturbed by dreams of Hunter. The future terrified her, but so also did the secret she was keeping from him.

Keisha had been living in Scotland for a little over two months when she'd made the startling discovery that she was pregnant. She had thought that her missed periods were due to the upheaval in her life, but when she'd visited a doctor because she wasn't feeling well he'd given her the news.

'But I can't be,' she shrieked. 'I don't want this child. I no longer love the father.'

'Things might change when you tell him you're pregnant,' said the doctor kindly. 'I've known it to happen.'

It took Keisha several days to get over the shock and to finally accept that she was carrying Hunter's baby, and a few more days before she convinced herself that she had to tell him. It was only right that he should know. But her heart was hammering fit to burst when she finally made the phone call.

Her relief knew no bounds when there was no answer. Not that day, nor for the next few days—which didn't really surprise her. He hadn't changed his lifestyle one iota. She could have tried his mobile, of course, or the office, but she didn't want to give him such personal information when he could be in a business meeting. They needed to talk—really talk—and decide on the future.

And then the unthinkable happened.

Keisha woke one morning, after a particularly unsettling dream, with violent pains in her stomach. So severe that she rang for an ambulance. Something was dreadfully wrong. She didn't know what, but she knew that her baby's life was in danger.

And in that moment, although she had initially told herself that she didn't want Hunter's child, she knew that she loved it more than life itself.

She fought the pains fiercely as she waited for the ambulance, and on arrival at the hospital she was rushed into an operating theatre.

When she came round she was given the sad news that she had lost her baby.

Keisha felt numb. She had gone from not wanting the child to wanting it desperately, and now she had lost it. How cruel was that?

The surgeon told her that she was a very lucky young woman because she had almost lost her own life as well.

'I don't call that lucky,' she told him with a wan smile.

'There were serious complications,' he said, and began telling her what had gone wrong, what the future might hold. 'I think it's highly unlikely,' he said, holding her hands, his eyes full of compassion, 'that you'll ever be able to have children. I'm sorry to have to tell you this, but it's—'

Keisha was too exhausted to listen properly. She let most of what he was saying pass over her head.

'Do you want me to send for anyone?' asked the surgeon gently.

Keisha shook her head.

'Your husband, maybe?'

'He's in London,' she said quietly, her voice shaking with emotion. 'I'll be all right.'

And in the days that followed, while she was recuperating, while she was regaining her strength and rebuilding her emotions, Keisha knew that there was no point now in telling Hunter about the baby.

They had been the saddest days of her life.

Keisha woke at six o'clock, disturbed by her dreams, worried about facing Hunter. She took a shower and dismissed breakfast, knowing she couldn't eat a thing, drinking cup after cup of coffee instead.

And when he arrived, bang on time, she was ready for him—at least as ready as she would ever be. She was understandably nervous, and when she saw him standing there, in a dark suit and pale blue shirt, looking dangerously threatening, she wanted to slam the door in his face. She wanted to run as far away from him as possible.

'Good—you're ready,' he said, his eyes running swiftly over the charcoal jacket and skirt she had thought eminently suitable for her new position. 'And you look every inch the part. Let's go.'

His offices had moved to the other side of London, and were now housed in a brand-new building. It was large and impressive and, to Keisha's relief, seemed to have a whole new army of staff. She had been dreading meeting anyone she had known before.

Alison, Hunter's assistant, was a very friendly woman, older than Keisha had thought—probably well into her thirties—and this was her first baby. She was terribly excited, and couldn't help talking about it, but she also took the time to ease Keisha into the job.

'Hunter's a wonderful man to work for,' she praised. 'You'll have no problem with him. He has a reputation for being something of a playboy, but I don't believe it for one minute. He's always been a proper gentleman to me.'

Keisha said nothing.

'So where did he find you?' probed Alison. 'He's exhausted all the agencies. No one came up to his expectations.'

'I suspect you've spoilt him,' said Keisha. 'Tell me again—where do these files go?' And she successfully avoided the question.

Hunter had told her on the way to the office that he had dealt with her landlord. 'Not a nice piece of work,' he remarked. 'I'll be happy when you move out of there.' But for the rest of the day she hardly saw him.

'He's such a busy man,' said Alison admiringly. 'I'm going to miss him.'

'But you are coming back?' asked Keisha with a frown.

'I've let him think so, Keisha, but in my heart of hearts I know I'm not going to be able to let anyone else look after this little fellow.' She patted her tummy proudly. 'I've waited so long for this baby; I want to enjoy every minute.'

Keisha felt a twinge of jealousy as she thought about the baby she had lost, and it was hard to push it to the back of her mind.

Six months had sounded like a lifetime working for Hunter, but she had convinced herself that she could stick it out. Not a day longer, though. She would be on her feet by then, and would easily be able to move on. But now Alison was saying that she wasn't coming back. Hunter would expect—no, demand of her that she fill the post permanently.

Towards the end of the day Hunter called her into his office. 'Alison says you're picking things up remarkably quickly,' he announced, with some degree of satisfaction. 'It looks as though you're going to settle into the job very well.'

'Thank you,' said Keisha, her hands demurely locked together in her lap, her hormones tightly tucked away.

'We do have one problem, though.'

She dragged her brows together, her eyes curious. She couldn't think what it might be.

'The question of transport,' he enlightened her. 'It would be my pleasure to pick you up and take you home each day but, as you will appreciate, it won't always be practical— unless, of course, you move in with me,' he added, one eyebrow lifted. 'No, I didn't think so,' he announced, when she sat that little bit straighter and looked prepared to do battle. 'So my suggestion is that I provide you with a car.'

Keisha's mouth fell open. 'You can't do that; you've already been more than generous. I can use the bus.'

'I wouldn't hear of it,' he retorted. 'I understand they're not always reliable. If I can't treat my ex-wife, considering that she's helping me out, then I'm not half the man I thought I was. It will be my pleasure, Keisha.'

His eyes locked into hers, daring her to refuse, but his voice was so carefully polite that Keisha wondered whether he was expecting something more of her. He wouldn't do all this for nothing, surely?

When she didn't answer he took it as a yes. His smile was wide. 'That's settled then. I'll have one delivered straight away.'

Keisha was lost for words. She didn't see how it was possible, and yet when she left the office an hour later a brand new car stood outside. Hunter escorted her to it.

'It's taxed and insured, and there's a tank full of petrol.' He dangled a set of keys in front of her.

'I don't know what to say,' she breathed. 'This is too much by far.'

'All I ask is that you prove the trust I'm putting in you,' he replied gravely.

'I'm sure I can do the job,' she said.

Hunter nodded. 'Then we'll both be happy.'

On Friday evening he called her into his office. He leaned back in his leather chair looking every inch the successful executive, and Keisha wondered what was coming. 'I thought we'd go out tomorrow,' he said. 'We'll have a trip down the Thames on my boat.'

She had expected him to say something about the job— ask how she was getting on—and she was completely taken aback. This was the last thing she wanted. Surely he didn't expect payment in kind for the money he'd lent her?

Keisha shuddered. She wouldn't put it past him. He was such a highly sexed individual that he wouldn't miss a single opportunity. And she had played right into his hands.

'I have shopping and washing to do,' she said quickly. 'And the house to clean. I'm sorry, I can't.'

'Such a little place,' he scorned. 'It won't take two minutes. Actually, I'm giving you no choice. I want you to spend tomorrow with me. Maybe Sunday as well. We still have a lot of catching up to do.'

'Are you telling me that you no longer work weekends?' asked Keisha, willing her heart to stop its stampede. This was ridiculous. He couldn't take up all of her time like this; she wouldn't let him.

'Only when there's nothing better to do,' he answered, with a smile on his lips and a twinkle in his eyes. 'And actually, Keisha, I think you owe me big-time. I don't think you're in any position to refuse.'

'That's blackmail!' she cried, heat rushing through her body like an avalanche.

Hunter shrugged. 'Call it what you like. I helped you out

of a desperate situation. I didn't have to do it. I could easily have turned my back on you.'

'And I can just as easily tell you where to stick your job,' countered Keisha. 'You cannot make demands on me like this.'

'Are you afraid of me?' Hunter's lips curled into an even wider smile.

Such smug confidence, she thought, wanting to knock it right off his face. 'Why should I be afraid?' she asked, squaring her shoulders, open defiance in her eyes.

'Something tells me you still have feelings.'

'For you?' she questioned crisply. 'Don't flatter yourself, Hunter. You're well and truly out of my system.'

Still he continued to smile. 'Deny it all you like, my pretty Keisha. Your body tells an entirely different story.'

'And you want me to spend the weekend with you so that you can prove it? Is that what you're suggesting?' Keisha was horrified that he had sensed she still felt a certain attraction. It wasn't something she was proud of; it was something she couldn't help.

He was such a physically exciting man that no woman in her right mind could ignore him. He might not have been a very caring husband—but he'd been the world's most exciting lover. Even now, thinking about it made her stomach curl into knots.

'I promise I won't ask anything of you that you don't want to give,' he said. But his eyes told a different story. He wanted her! Big-time!

'And I suspect that promise will go the same way as all those you made about keeping more regular working hours!' she challenged.

Hunter lifted broad shoulders and let them drop again. 'You have to trust me, Keisha.'

'If I want to keep the job? Is that what you're saying?' she flared. Lord, he really had got her where he wanted her.

'Something like that.'

'In other words I have no choice. I spend tomorrow with you, or it's back to temping.'

'I wouldn't put it quite so crudely,' he said.

'But it's what you mean all the same,' she snapped. 'OK, I'll do it.' She had to say it quickly, before she ruined her chances of getting back on her own two feet. It would have been so easy to tell him what he could do with his job.

In actual fact he'd got her where he wanted her.

She hadn't thought of this before; she'd been so grateful for his job offer that she hadn't seen any pitfalls. And she couldn't help wondering now why he wanted to spend even more time with her. Any normal man would steer clear of an ex-wife.

But she already knew, didn't she, that Hunter wasn't like other men? He had always worked hard, and now it looked as though he was reaping the rewards of his labours by playing hard as well.

'I'll send a car for you,' he said.

'I can drive myself,' insisted Keisha. She wanted to be able to leave when she felt like it, not remain until Hunter decided that he'd had enough of her.

But he wouldn't hear of it. 'Shall we say about ten?'

She nodded, not trusting herself to speak.

'One last thing,' said Hunter as she got up from her chair.

Keisha groaned inwardly. Now what?

'I'd just like to say how pleased I am with the way you're coping. Not that I expected anything less from you.'

A warm glow replaced Keisha's resentment. 'Thank you,' she said simply.

'Are you enjoying the work?'

She nodded.

'And I'm enjoying you working for me. Crazy as it sounds, I've missed you, Keisha.'

Oh, Lord! It definitely sounded as though he was going to spend the entire weekend trying to persuade her back into his bed.

CHAPTER FIVE

KEISHA WAS READY when the car came for her, but she wasn't ready for the warmth of Hunter's reception. He came to greet her almost before she had stepped out of the car, folding her in his arms as though she was still his wife and had been away for a long time.

When he tried to kiss her, however, she turned her head. This was taking things too far. She had lain awake worrying that it would be a big mistake spending a whole day with him, and now she knew that her fears were justified.

It was impossible to ignore the heat prickling her skin, the tightness threatening her throat. Was it to be this way for the rest of her life? she wondered. Was she never to get over him? Would he always have the power to arouse her most basic instincts?

She wanted to turn tail and run, but it was out of the question. The heavy iron gates had closed behind the chauffeur-driven Bentley as soon as they'd driven through them. She was Hunter's prisoner. It wasn't until this precise moment that she'd realised it.

He had planned everything down to the last detail.

She was his now—to do with as he liked.

To punish for daring to run away from him.

Maybe even to make love to!

To fulfil some very basic needs in himself.

Keisha felt a shiver of something akin to fear. Never had she dreamt that she would be frightened of Hunter. But she was. Afraid of the feelings he aroused in her. Afraid that she wouldn't be able to control them, to resist him.

Whatever happened between them, though, she knew that they had no future. She would never go back to him. Never! Not to the sort of life that he led. He might be taking time off now, but that was because he wanted something from her. A leopard never changed its spots. Wasn't that what they said? It had to be true about Hunter.

He led her towards the house. 'Have you had breakfast?'

'Just some coffee. I wasn't hungry.'

'Then it's no wonder you're so thin,' he declared. 'Come, I'll get my cook to rustle you something up.'

'Please, no,' insisted Keisha, but he took not the slightest bit of notice.

'I can't have you fainting on me,' he said, leading her into a small breakfast room. It had a table for two in front of the window, with a view of the river, and Keisha couldn't help wondering who else had shared it with him.

'I won't be long,' he promised.

Left alone she was able to breathe more easily. But the thought of an entire day spent in Hunter's company sat heavily on her shoulders. When he returned she wanted to demand that he take her home.

Of course she didn't.

For one thing she knew he wouldn't, and for another it would alert him to how uncomfortable she felt. And she didn't want him to know that. She wanted him to believe that she was capable of handling the situation, that she was more mature now in her outlook on life. It was only this man who managed to stir her senses to such an extent that she didn't know which way she was going.

'So how have you been sleeping?' he asked, taking the seat opposite her. 'I have to confess after the shock of bumping into you again like that I've had trouble sleeping myself. My thoughts are all over the place.'

This didn't sound like Hunter; he was not one to admit to his innermost thoughts. But if he felt that by acknowledging his own demons she might tell him about hers, he was sorely mistaken.

'I have no trouble sleeping,' she lied. 'This is a lovely room.' She'd glimpsed some of them as he led her though the house—monstrous rooms that were distinctly uninviting. 'The others looked too big to be comfortable, though I can understand why you need them if you hold meetings here.'

'Meetings I shall expect you to attend,' he announced gravely.

Keisha frowned, her heart stammering at an alarming rate. The situation was getting worse by the minute. 'Why?'

'Because you'll need to take minutes—it's part of the job, Keisha. Didn't Alison tell you that?'

'I guess she didn't get around to it,' she muttered.

'It doesn't please you?'

'What do you think?' she snapped, suddenly unable to help herself. 'I suppose you'd expect me to stay here if it's a weekend conference?'

'Naturally.' His voice was so casual that Keisha couldn't help feeling suspicious. He'd obviously had all this in mind when he'd offered to help her out. Whereas all she'd thought was that she'd be doing a nine-to-five job at the office. He'd fooled her good and proper.

Maybe he had helped her financially, and she would be in his debt for a long time, but all these add-ons were making her very uncomfortable.

Keisha was grateful when her breakfast arrived, though in point of fact she didn't feel that she could eat a thing. She sipped her orange juice, she pecked at the bacon and egg, nibbled at a slice of toast, but didn't do the food justice at all. How could she when he was hammering blow after blow on her?

Hunter, on the other hand, was totally relaxed. He sat back and sipped his coffee, watching her through narrowed lids, the curl of his lips seeming to suggest that he was amused by her discomfiture.

Which he probably was.

But what he was trying to achieve by demanding so much of her company she really couldn't think. Could he be trying to get his own back? Hurt her in some way, as she had hurt him? She dismissed the thought as unworthy. Hunter wouldn't stoop to such measures.

She was genuinely confused by what he did want from her, though—and not a little unhappy at her own feelings. Which were mixed, to say the least. He still had the power to hold her in his thrall, but the other half of her wanted to bail out right there and then. There was no future for them together, if that was what he had in mind. No chance of a reconciliation. Of that she was very sure.

Finally, with breakfast over, they walked down to the water's edge. He took her elbow, and Keisha was forced to keep up. She could feel the heat of his body, and even sense the male hormones running rampant inside him. She was heading for trouble—and for the moment there was no way out of it.

His cabin cruiser wasn't large, but it had beautiful sleek lines and looked as though it had cost a lot of money. Most astonishing of all, though, was its name. *Keisha!*

'You named it after me?' she asked. 'Why?'

Hunter smiled wryly. 'Because it reminds me of you. It's totally unpredictable.'

'You can't be serious?'

'I am,' he said. 'It's jinxed. It has a mind of its own. I'm thinking of buying a new one. Maybe I'll call that *Keisha* as well. What do you think?'

'I think you're crazy,' she declared.

Hunter smiled, a secretive little smile that set her nerves on edge. Soon they were cruising down the river, and it would have been relaxing if it hadn't been for the man at her side. No matter how she tried, she could not ignore his sexuality.

It had been a big mistake, allowing herself to be cajoled into this trip. There was no escape—none at all. She was forced to drink in the very essence of him, to stand close enough to feel the electric force of him.

Did he feel the same? she wondered. Was he too experiencing vibes from the past? Was it his intention to have his way with her down there in the cabin, where no one would disturb them? She shivered.

Immediately Hunter looked concerned. 'Are you cold?'

Keisha shook her head. 'Just someone walking over my grave.'

'Like an ex-husband, perhaps?'

Disturbed by his perspicacity, Keisha looked away.

'Have you had any regrets?' he queried softly.

'Absolutely not,' she retorted, loudly and plainly. 'Leaving you was the best thing I ever did.' And she meant it. Remaining married would have meant a lifetime's misery.

Hunter's lips thinned and he didn't answer. Keisha guessed it was because *she* had walked out on him and not the other way round. He didn't like to think that he wasn't Mr Perfection. But he should have thought of that a long time ago. She'd complained enough. If he hadn't seen what he was doing to her then he'd been very blind indeed.

By lunchtime, however, they had both relaxed in each other's company, and Keisha found that she was enjoying herself far more than she had ever imagined. Hunter had made no untoward advances, he had been friendly and talkative—though not about anything personal—and all in all she was glad that she had come. She was even feeling hungry!

He tied up outside an inn, and Keisha realised once they were inside that it was the same one he had taken her to on their very first date. Was it a coincidence, or deliberate? She didn't dare ask. What it did was bring back memories of the lovestruck teenager she had been then. She had thought herself so grown-up, being wined and dined by this great man. Little had she known that it would all end in misery.

The restaurant had been upgraded, and was very busy, but the moment Hunter walked in he was found a table.

'You eat here often?' she asked.

'They're customers of mine,' he told her casually. 'At least the group is, to which they belong.'

'And consequently you get preferential treatment?'

His face darkened fractionally. 'You sound as though it upsets you, Keisha. Do you have a problem with it?'

Keisha shrugged. 'I'm beginning to realise how much you've gone up in the world. Being successful opens a lot of doors, doesn't it?'

'I suppose it does,' he answered quietly.

'You mean you take it for granted?' she tossed back, not

meaning to sound resentful but unable to help herself. She was not resentful of his success, merely the toll it had taken on their marriage.

'Sour grapes don't become you, Keisha,' he said sharply, and picked up his menu.

The food was superb, but Hunter's mood didn't change. It was her own fault, thought Keisha; she shouldn't have baited him. She couldn't wait to get home now—to put an end to this farce of pretending to be happy in each other's company. Again she couldn't help wondering why he was insisting on her spending so much time with him. It didn't suit either of them. Surely he knew that? She was beginning to realise that, despite being married to Hunter for a whole year, she really didn't know him very well at all.

On the trip back to his house they were both silent, and once there Keisha was in such a hurry to get off the boat that she completely missed her footing. With a horrified cry she slipped into the river. The water was cold, and she was embarrassed—especially when Hunter jumped in to help her out.

'You didn't have to do that,' she protested, alarmed that his touch should trigger sensations she wanted to forget. Her jeans were mud-stained and her seersucker top clung reverently to her breasts. Something that Hunter did not fail to notice.

He was smiling now, amused by her distress. 'What were you doing? Trying to run away from me? You leapt off the boat as though I was about to attack you.'

'Considering I didn't want to be here in the first place, is it surprising?' she asked.

'And now you're in an even darker mood because you feel foolish.'

'Go to hell!' she snapped.

'Not a place I would enjoy,' he countered. 'What we both need is a shower and a change of clothes.'

'Ha, ha—very funny! I don't have any with me.'

'I'm sure I can find you something,' said Hunter smoothly, 'while my housekeeper launders your things.'

Keisha did not want to wear anything of Hunter's. She had in the past. His shirt first thing in the morning, when she felt a bit chilly before taking her shower, for instance. Sometimes she had walked around in it all day—that and nothing else!

But to do so now would be far too intimate. She didn't know what he'd had in mind when he suggested they spend the day together, but what she hadn't expected was to be wearing his clothes.

'So what are you going to do? Sit around in the nude?' he asked calmly.

Keisha tossed her head and stamped away towards the house. Then had to wait until he caught her up because she wasn't sure where to go.

He led her to one of the bedrooms, provided her with towels and a robe, and then left her to it. Keisha thought he was being very kind—until she heard him singing in another shower right next door.

He was far too close for comfort. Her vivid imagination could see him standing there naked, could see every inch of his magnificent body.

Was he thinking about her too? Was that why he had chosen adjoining rooms? Was he singing because he was happy that she was in his power and there was nothing she could do about it?

She jumped out of the shower and towelled herself dry before pulling on the robe he had provided. A woman's robe.

It didn't surprise her, but she didn't like the thought that some other female had worn it before her. Someone who had shared Hunter's bed! She didn't believe for one moment that he'd remained celibate.

Curiously she opened a wardrobe door and peeped inside—and felt instant relief when it held nothing but male clothing.

'Looking for something to wear?'

She jumped at the sound of Hunter's voice. 'What the hell are you doing here?' He wasn't even wearing a robe, just a towel around his loins. Her heart broke into an amazing flutter. He was more muscular than she'd imagined, and his skin was beautifully tanned. She had a brief impulse to touch, to feel that polished skin just one more time, and then berated herself for being stupid.

She would be walking right into his hands, and the next thing she knew she'd be tumbling into his bed. Her stomach crunched at the thought, and she flared hot eyes in his direction.

'I came to see if you had everything you needed.'

'As you can see, I'm fine,' she retorted sharply.

'You're comfortable in the robe?'

She nodded.

'So what were you looking for?'

Keisha winced. 'I wondered whose room this was.'

'In other words you were being nosy?' But there was no malice in his words; indeed a tiny, satisfied smile curved the corners of his mouth. 'Give me your clothes, and I'll take them down to Helen.'

Keisha was glad to move away, to hide her overheated cheeks, and as she gathered up her sodden clothes she wondered exactly why he'd come into the room dressed as he was. Surely he would have put something on if he were intending to go downstairs?

Perhaps he'd been hoping?

Her lips tightened. Not in this lifetime!

But even so she couldn't ignore the way her body had leapt into life at the sight of all that naked flesh.

She wrapped her wet clothing in a towel and dumped it in his arms as quickly as she could. He'd moved further into the room, giving her the impression that he was in no hurry to leave. Thank goodness his hands were now occupied.

As Hunter turned Keisha breathed a sigh of relief, but it was short-lived when he said, 'Don't run away. I'll be back in a minute.'

Back for what? she mused. What did people usually do in bedrooms? She had no intention of waiting to find out. As soon as he was out of sight she made her way downstairs and through a pair of doors to the terrace. The sun was warm, and she turned her face up to it as she sat down and closed her eyes.

She was still sitting like that when Hunter came to find her. She sensed his presence rather than heard his footsteps. He'd never been someone you could ignore, but now he had a much more powerful charisma.

'What are you doing out here?' His voice was a rough growl, as though he was annoyed that she hadn't waited in the bedroom. His feet were bare and he was still wearing only the towel.

'Enjoying the sunshine. Do you have a problem with it?'

'But I told you to—'

'I know what you said,' interrupted Keisha quickly. 'But what was the point? Unless, of course, you had something— in mind?' She paused before adding sharply, 'Let me tell you right now, Hunter, I'm not up for anything like that.'

'And what would that be, exactly?' he asked, his eyes un-faltering on hers.

Keisha lifted her chin even higher. 'I don't think I need spell it out in words. Why else would you remain dressed like—that?'

Hunter smiled, and to her horror whipped off his towel.

Relief flooded her when she saw that he was wearing a pair of black swim shorts.

'Did I show you my pool?' he asked innocently.

Her smile was faint. 'No, you did not.'

'Care to join me?'

'No, thank you,' she replied. 'But you go. I'm quite enjoying sitting here.'

'You could come and watch at least.'

And torture herself with his beautiful body? She didn't think so. 'No, I'm all right.'

'Suit yourself,' he said with a shrug. 'But you don't know what you're missing.'

A few minutes later curiosity got the better of her, and Keisha wandered in the direction he had taken. The pool was in a purpose built conservatory on the side of the house, where palms and other exotic plants grew, and Hunter seemed to be punishing himself by doing a very fast crawl.

It was not until he turned and was halfway back again that he saw her. Immediately he swam to her side. 'Can't I persuade you to change your mind? It's lovely in here.'

Keisha would have liked nothing better than to use the pool—the water looked very enticing—but modesty prevailed. 'I don't think so,' she said. 'I was just curious, that's all.'

But Hunter had other ideas. He shot up out of the water like a dolphin doing tricks, and pulled her back down with him. Her robe came undone as if by magic, and he wasted no time in pulling it off her.

All that surrounded her was warm silken water—and Hunter's prying eyes.

Keisha swam away from Hunter as swiftly and strongly as she could. She ought to have known what would happen. She could feel her whole body tingling with need. As strong as it had ever been.

It was a fearful feeling, and she wished there was some way out; she wished that she had never let her curiosity get the better of her. She ought to have stayed in her chair; she ought not to have ventured here to this pool—where Hunter was waiting to pounce.

More than that she wished that she had never let Gillian persuade her to go to that party. If her friend had had any idea...

'There's no escape.'

Hunter's voice growled in her ear, and Keisha felt further alarm bells clang. He swam easily at her side, rolling on to his back so that he could look at her, kicking with his legs, moving his hands gently like flippers.

Keisha veered away, but he reached out and caught her arm, pulling her towards him. The water was shallow enough for them to stand, but when his arms made her his prisoner, when his mouth swooped down, intent on claiming hers, Keisha ducked out of his embrace and swam as hard as she could to the other end of the pool.

'Don't you dare,' she yelled, turning to see that he was still standing where she had left him.

He didn't look angry, though, or even disappointed. Instead a great big smile split his face. 'What are you scared of, my little pussycat?'

'Not you,' she retorted, wishing there was a dignified way out of this situation.

'So if it's not me, then it must be your own feelings.'

Damn! She had walked right into that one. 'You had no right taking advantage.'

'Would I do that?' he asked, and to her alarm he began swimming slowly towards her.

Hurriedly she began to haul herself out. It was a question of saving her virtue or her modesty, and she decided virtue was paramount. But Hunter was too swift. He caught up with her before she'd made it, pulling her back down into the luxurious warm water.

As he imprisoned her against him, as he swam to where they could comfortably stand, all energy and fight suddenly went out of her. She became aware only of feelings too intense to describe. And as his mouth swooped down on hers she was powerless to stop him.

She really had thought all her feelings were dead, but here in this pool, with the silky water caressing her skin, with Hunter's expert mouth coaxingly on hers, every single one of them revived. Her resistance fled like a bird on the wing. She no longer had any fight left in her.

His kisses reminded her of past pleasures.

And past unhappiness!

What was she thinking? Why had she let herself get caught up like this? 'Get away from me, Hunter,' she yelled, pushing against him with all her might.

He smiled, a slow satisfied smile that set her teeth on edge. 'You don't mean that, Keisha.' And his arms tightened around her.

'Oh, yes, I do,' she retorted furiously. 'You're taking advantage. You can't bear the thought that I walked out on you, can you? It's your stupid male pride that's at stake here.'

'If that's what you care to think,' he said, with a shrug. 'Actually, I get the impression that you're really rather enjoying my kisses.' And with that remark he bowed his head to hers again.

CHAPTER SIX

IT DIDN'T BOTHER Hunter that he still found Keisha extremely
desirable. He'd always had a high sex drive, and when he'd
met her all those years ago he had been delighted to discover
that her appetite was as healthy as his. He had enjoyed
teaching her, seeing the way she embraced making love, the
way she sometimes took the initiative.

And he would enjoy using her body now. For sex was all
it would be. Love didn't enter into the equation any more.

'I'm not enjoying your kisses,' Keisha declared, staring at
him disbelievingly. 'How can you say that when you're
kissing me against my will?'

'Really?' He locked his eyes into her beautiful green ones.
They were such a unique colour, unlike any other he had ever
seen. Sometimes aquamarine, sometimes pea-green, sometimes emerald. All depending on her mood. At this moment
they were an even different colour, as reflections from the
water mingled with her anger.

'Yes, against my will,' she reaffirmed.

'I didn't see you struggling.' In fact he could have sworn
that she was enjoying the kiss as much as he was.

Keisha gave him a magnificent glare. 'There's not really
much point—not against you.'

'I'll take that as a compliment,' he said with a smile.

'I want to get out of here,' she declared icily.

His smile widened. 'What's stopping you?' Although he knew what her answer was going to be.

'You are!' she snapped. 'I'd appreciate it if you'd turn your back.'

He allowed his brows to ride up smoothly. 'I've seen everything a million times before—although I have to admit there was more of you. I'm concerned by the weight you've lost, Keisha. It's unhealthy. You didn't have to pine over me quite so much,' he added, with a quirk of his lips.

She shot him a disdainful glare. 'As if! It was looking after my mother that did this to me.'

'I'm sorry,' he said at once. And he meant it.

He swam away from her, giving her a moment to compose herself. And when he next looked she was out of the pool and the wet robe was back in place. He couldn't help but admire her spirit, and guilt flickered through him again. He should have been with her to share the burden.

'Looks like I need to find you something else to wear,' he said, hauling himself out and joining her. 'There's a changing room just to the side there. You'll find plenty of towels. Help yourself.'

When she emerged a few minutes later, with a large, brightly patterned towel wrapped tightly around her, he was struck anew by how pathetically thin she had become. And he wanted to do something about it!

But looking after her, helping her become the woman he had once known, wasn't in his plan of things at all, and he felt swift anger at himself. 'I'll go and see how long your clothes will be,' he announced, and headed indoors.

Damn! He didn't want to feel concern. He didn't want to

feel anything but rage over the way she had treated him. He checked on her clothes, then retired to his study and spent almost an hour poring over papers without any real idea of what he was doing.

The next thing he knew Keisha was knocking on his door, and when he bade her enter she was dressed again in her close-fitting jeans and the thin top that clung slavishly to her too tempting breasts.

'Sit down,' he said brusquely, pushing away the sudden urge to touch her.

Keisha shook her head. 'I want to go home.'

'You've had enough of me for today? Is that it?'

She nodded.

And he knew he mustn't rush things—no matter how much he wanted to. But at least he had reached a better understanding of her. He knew for a fact that she wasn't immune to him, that there were very real feelings dancing around inside her. Of which he intended taking full advantage!

But one step at a time.

Perhaps tomorrow he'd give her a reprieve—let her come to terms with the fact that her body still hungered for his, that her sex hormones didn't die at the sight of him but instead rose up in all their glory.

And then at the office on Monday he'd carry on his insidious attack on her defences. The thought gave him great pleasure. There was only one fly in the ointment. Today he had felt a faint surge of feeling for her. Nothing much, but enough to warn him to be on his guard. He could be wrong, of course. He hoped he was wrong. He wanted nothing that would ruin his grand plan.

Keisha had very mixed feelings as she made her way to the office on Monday morning. She had spent all day Sunday wondering whether she had made a fool of herself, whether she had unintentionally given away to Hunter the fact that he still had the power to disturb her.

And if she had would he take advantage?

It really did concern her that he could so easily arouse her feelings. Was she being a fool, or was this just a normal reaction to someone as sexy as Hunter? Despite the fact that he was the man who had let her down so badly? If she wanted to be honest with herself she had let him down as well.

Monday and Tuesday passed without hitch. Alison had gone off on her maternity leave and he was in full work mode, keeping her so busy that she hardly had time to think.

Nevertheless Keisha was soon made very much aware that everything he was doing for her came with a price! And it was at a far higher price than she had ever imagined.

'You can't be serious?' Keisha stared at Hunter in wide-eyed astonishment.

'Oh, but I am.'

'You expect me to move abroad with you?'

'Absolutely. It's a condition of the job.'

'But you said nothing about that when you offered me work.'

Hunter's smile was wickedly confident. 'Would you have taken it if I had?'

Keisha shook her head. 'Never in my wildest dreams.'

'There you are, then,' he said. 'I did you a favour. You're out of debt, you're in work, and you're going to spend the winter in the sun. What more could you ask for?'

Keisha closed her eyes and shook her head. Just when she had thought everything was going swimmingly. 'I couldn't ask for anything more,' she answered tightly, shooting him a venomous green stare. 'But I don't want to go to Spain!'

It was a ridiculous suggestion. She knew that Hunter had business interests in Europe, but never for one moment had she dreamt that he had a home there as well. He'd kept that a secret.

And Alison had said nothing about it either!

'You have no choice, Keisha.' Hunter's tone was suddenly serious. 'We're leaving at the weekend. Your passport is in order?'

She nodded miserably. The matter was being taken out of her hands. She could either start looking for work again, or accompany Hunter to Spain.

'Wh-where would I live?' she asked faintly.

'With me, of course,' came the swift answer. 'But don't worry—it's a big enough house for you to have your own space.'

And as far as he was concerned the matter was settled.

For the rest of the week Keisha was tortured by thoughts of living with Hunter again. Own space or not, they would be under the same roof. There would be no escaping him.

But what option did she have?

She needed to pay off her debt to Hunter. He had tried to refuse any money, but Keisha had been adamant. And she wouldn't be happy until she had paid back every last penny.

When Saturday morning came Keisha was as nervous as a kitten. Only one thing was she certain of—she wouldn't allow any sort of intimacy between them. No more kisses, no more touching. Nothing. It would be far too dangerous—especially with a man like Hunter.

Hunter by name, hunter by nature! She would need to be on her guard at all times.

Start as you mean to go on, she told herself firmly.

The first hint of disaster came on the flight over. It was a private jet—whether it was Hunter's or not Keisha had no idea—but it was certainly too cosy for comfort. There was no escaping him.

'I've told your landlord that you won't be needing the house any longer,' announced Hunter calmly as he handed her a glass of wine. 'I gave him a month's rent in lieu of notice.'

'You did what?' questioned Keisha loudly, almost dropping the glass. 'How dare you? That's my home. All my belongings are there. You can't do this to me!'

'So you'd rather pay rent for six months to a man who's no more than a crook?' he asked sharply. 'You'd rather the house sit there empty? Lord knows what might happen to it. I wouldn't trust that man not to move someone else in.'

Keisha had to confess that she had been worried about leaving it, but since she'd been given no choice in the matter she'd had to push her fears to the back of her mind. Now, though, she was furious. 'But my stuff—all my personal things, all my mother's furniture! What's going to happen to them?' she questioned frantically. Lord, did this man stop at anything?

Hunter put a hand on her arm. 'You have nothing to fear.' His voice was low and encouraging. 'I'm having everything put into storage. You can sort it when we get home.'

Keisha dashed his hand away. 'How dare you take control of my life?' If they hadn't been in the air she would have walked away from him. For ever! Gone as far as she could get. Back to Scotland, probably. Somewhere he would never find her.

She was so angry with him! 'You really have gone too far, Hunter. I never wanted to come to Spain with you, and now I wish I'd stuck to my guns. You're a manipulative, scheming bastard. And I hate you!'

'No, you don't.' His voice was gentle; he was even smiling.

Smiling because he'd got his own way. Lord, she wanted to kick him where it hurt.

'You might think so at this moment,' he went on, 'but one day you'll thank me for it.'

'Thank *you?*' she cried. 'I don't think so. Not ever!' Could he really be trying to settle a score? Was this his way of making her suffer for walking out on him? She didn't want to think so, but it was beginning to look more and more likely.

Most definitely she would need to be on her guard for every second of every day. Six months was going to be a lifetime.

She tossed the contents of her wine glass down her throat in a couple of swallows. She needed it. She needed something to dull her mind to what she'd landed herself in for.

'More wine?' Hunter asked pleasantly.

She held out her glass, and drank that down quickly too, but he offered her no more. He merely sat and studied her, with a quiet smile playing on his lips.

Keisha was glad when they touched down. But her relief was short-lived when she was compelled to sit with Hunter in the back of a chauffeur-driven Mercedes. She resolutely kept her head turned away from him, pretending to study the landscape but in effect seeing nothing at all.

When they eventually pulled up outside a magnificent villa built high on the top of a hill, she couldn't wait to get out of the car.

'You look like a scared little rabbit,' he said softly as he came to stand beside her. 'You really have nothing to worry about.'

'Perhaps not in your eyes,' she retorted.

'I'm showing you a different world.'

'I know,' she said quietly. 'And under any other circumstances I'd be grateful. But you and I living together, working together, is not going to work, is it?'

His eyes darkened beneath the hot Mediterranean sun. 'We could make it work.' And there was a depth of meaning behind his words that sent a cold shiver down Keisha's spine. She wasn't sure what he was suggesting, but she felt quite sure that he wasn't talking solely about work.

'Come,' he said, taking her elbow. 'Let me show you my house.'

'But my luggage—' she complained faintly, already knowing that her protest was in vain.

'Someone will see to that. Don't worry your pretty little head about it.'

His grip on her arm was secure, and Keisha began to feel that she was his prisoner. She might not have bars to hold her, but Hunter was without a doubt her jailer. She clenched her teeth, curled her fingers into damp palms, and tension tightened like a band of steel around her forehead.

'Relax,' said Hunter, smiling down at her. 'You should be enjoying this.'

'Did you bring Alison out here?' she asked huskily, and wasn't surprised when he said no.

'So it's not really part of the job, is it?' she asked harshly. 'It's something you thought up just for me.'

'Not at all,' he said. 'I have an office in Seville, and usually one of the secretaries there does my work. This year I thought I'd have a change. I've set up an office here at the villa. I thought it would be a perfect opportunity for you to enjoy some sunshine and build yourself up again.'

Keisha frowned. 'You mean I'm not going to work?'

'Of course you're going to work,' he answered quickly.

'But not all day every day! I shall enjoy taking you out and about. Have you ever been to Spain before?'

She nodded. 'I went with a friend to Alicante.'

Hunter frowned and his nostrils flared. 'Would that be a male friend? Perhaps even the male friend you used to see at the gym?'

Keisha looked at him sharply, wondering where this line of questioning had come from. 'I don't consider it any of your business,' she said shortly.

'I see.'

His faint smile told her that he thought she was hiding the fact that her companion had been male. In fact it had been her friend, Gillian. But she hadn't enjoyed the holiday because all Gillian had been interested in was the opposite sex. It was all she was ever interested in. Keisha wished that she'd meet some nice man who'd tame her and marry her.

But if Hunter thought that this conversation about whether she'd been to Spain or not would make her forget the fact that she was to live and work with him, he wasn't succeeding.

As they climbed the steps leading up to an arched doorway fear as thick and syrupy as treacle filled her throat. There was no going back now. She was here whether she liked it or not. She was dependent solely upon this man.

The inside of the villa was superb. Cool and spacious and airy. And she knew that under any other circumstances she would have loved it.

From the outside Keisha had noticed that there were three floors, each one smaller than the one below, so that they rose in tiers like a wedding cake. Except that there was nothing sickly-sweet about this place. It was handsome—very handsome indeed.

The outer walls were painted cream and terracotta, with

terracotta pantiled roofs, but indoors everything was white. The only splashes of colour were in the pictures on the walls, in vases, and in the cushions on the white linen sofas and chairs.

It was very minimalist, and almost masculine, but not quite. There was a woman's touch here somewhere. On the ground floor was a massive living area, as well as a kitchen to die for. The dining room opened out on to a terrace at the back, overlooking the sea, and there was also another smaller sitting room that, she thought, could be used as a haven of peace if you wanted to get away from it all.

'What do you think of it so far?' asked Hunter as they walked side by side up a wide marble staircase.

'It's—er—very nice,' she acknowledged.

Hunter's brows rose. 'Is that all you have to say? Very nice?'

Keisha shrugged. 'OK, it's lovely. I like the fact that you haven't overfilled it with furniture.'

'Not like your tiny little home, eh?'

There was no offence meant and none taken. 'We could fit my whole house into your living area,' she admitted with a wry smile. 'But you have to admit it was cosy. You couldn't say that about this place.'

'I guess not,' he agreed. 'But perhaps you ought to wait until you've seen the bedrooms.'

Keisha felt a shiver of apprehension run down her spine. But she refused to let it show. And when Hunter pushed open the door to what she presumed was his room she was pleasantly surprised to see that it too was of spacious proportions.

Again everything was white—floor tiles, walls, ceiling, curtains, bedlinen—everything except for the gothic arched bedhead, which was black. 'You like white, do you?' she asked curiously. And then noticed that there were other touches of black in the room as well. Tiebacks, picture frames, a couple of statues.

'I gave my interior designer *carte blanche* and this is what she came up with. She must have thought me virginal,' he added, with a hint of humour in his voice.

'Then she didn't know you very well,' retorted Keisha. 'Which is my room?'

She was relieved to find that her accommodation was on the other side of the house. It was a much smaller room than Hunter's, and the white furnishings were relieved by pale lilac pillow trims, and lilac tiebacks for the curtains at the tall arched windows. It had its own dressing room, and a bathroom to die for.

She turned to him with a wide smile on her face. 'I love this. It's out of this world.'

'I'm pleased. I thought you'd like this room. Open that door over there.'

To her surprise it led out on to a private balcony, with cane chairs and a table and a potted plant or two for good measure. It overlooked the Mediterranean, and reminded her of the hotel where they'd spent their honeymoon.

Hunter was watching her face closely, and she wondered whether he too was thinking the same thing. Remembering when they'd stood naked and watched the sun go down. Remembering what had happened afterwards.

She turned swiftly back into the room. 'So where is the office?'

He gave a private little smile, leaving her in no doubt that he'd followed the same train of thought. 'Follow me.'

Up a spiral staircase they went this time, to a room that was perfectly square with windows on all sides. Keisha's initial impression was that it was like an observatory, but then she looked at all the expensive equipment and knew without a doubt that it was a very dedicated office.

'You could run an empire from here,' she muttered. There were two desks face to face: one for him, and one for whomever he chose to work with him. There would be no escape. Nevertheless it was a fantastic room, with far-reaching views over the surrounding countryside.

'So how do you rate it?' he asked.

Keisha suddenly realised that he had been watching her expression closely. 'Perfect!' was all she managed.

'I'm glad you approve,' he acknowledged drily. 'I suggest we go down now, and take a drink on the terrace. Something to eat wouldn't go amiss either.'

'But my bags? I need to unpack,' protested Keisha, feeling a strong need to get away from him for a few minutes. She'd had no choice but to breathe him in during the flight and she wanted some reprieve. No matter how short.

'Everything will be done for you,' he told her. 'Come, let's go and sit outside.'

Marvelling at the lifestyle he had created for himself, Keisha reluctantly followed. All this in three short years. It was nothing short of miraculous. Although not entirely surprising, considering that he had always been one step ahead of his competitors. Always the one with the innovative ideas. A real go-getter!

How it had paid off!

This was luxury. This was living. And for the next six months she was going to be part of it.

CHAPTER SEVEN

HUNTER FELT PARTICULARLY happy with himself. He'd had his doubts as to how Keisha would react when he demanded she join him here in Spain. Now he was looking forward to spending the next few months in her company.

Deliberately he had given her a bedroom as far away from his as possible in this villa he loved so much, but it was not his intention that she sleep there. Oh, no, he had far different ideas. He wanted her company in *his* bed.

They were served chilled juice, and a basket of crisp rolls with a platter of ham, sardines and tomatoes, and he was pleased when Keisha tucked in as though she were starving. He really was concerned with the weight she'd lost, and hoped that out here in this beautiful part of Spain she would have a healthy appetite and regain the voluptuous figure he had loved so much.

'Are you feeling better?' he asked, when she finally dabbed her mouth with a napkin and settled back in her chair.

'I didn't realise I was so hungry,' she answered, smiling into his eyes.

It pleased him that she no longer seemed to resent him flying her out here; in fact she was the most relaxed he had seen her since the party.

'So what's your plan of action?' asked Keisha. 'When do I start work?'

'Whoa!' he said, wondering if he had miscalculated her apparent ease. 'Don't rush things.'

'But—I understood this was purely a business arrangement?' A faint frown marred her brow, and her lovely green eyes were suddenly disturbed.

'It is,' he concurred, 'but no one works all of the time. Today we will simply rest. Maybe take a swim later, if you'd like that. I didn't show you the pool, did I?'

Keisha shook her head, but he could see that she was no longer happy with the situation. She didn't want a friendly relationship with him.

In that case she was in for a shock. Friendly was what he was going to be—in a big way. So friendly that her body wouldn't be able to resist him, that all her old feelings would come tumbling back with a vengeance.

Leaving him to take full advantage.

And when her fall came it would give him the greatest pleasure of all.

Keisha felt that she was being manipulated. Admittedly she couldn't work twenty-four seven, but it didn't mean that she had to spend her spare time with Hunter. She was here as his personal assistant; she was here to do a job. Not to fraternise with the enemy.

'You don't have to make it your duty to keep me entertained,' she told him crisply. 'Feel free to do whatever you like. There must be people you know here—people you'd rather see.'

Hunter smiled slowly, one of those smiles that had used to curl her insides and make her jump into his arms. She might even have been the one to instigate a long, satisfying love session. But not any longer.

'At this moment,' he said, 'there is no one I'd rather be looking at than you. You always were beautiful, Keisha. And you still are.'

'Flattery will get you nowhere,' she retorted quickly, squashing the fizz of sensation that had just danced through her veins.

'It's not flattery. I'm simply telling the truth as I see it.'

'You're my employer.' she remonstrated. 'You shouldn't be talking to me like this.'

'I'm also your ex-husband. Surely that stands for something?'

'*Ex* being the operative word,' she reminded him. He seemed to be suggesting that it gave him some sort of hold over her. That perhaps it even gave him the right to resume their relationship. Not in a thousand years!

Hunter smiled a long, slow smile that set her teeth on edge. 'I love it when you're angry,' he said. 'It brings your face to life and makes you look extremely sexy.'

Keisha sprang to her feet, resenting the compliment—if that was what it was. 'I'm going to take a shower and change my clothes, and I'd prefer not to see you again today.'

When she reached her room she was in a flat panic. If Hunter had it in mind to make love to her there was not a lot she could do about it. Her mind would fight, yes, but her body would be treacherously weak.

She stepped beneath the shower and closed her eyes, letting the water rain over her, hopefully washing away her uneasy thoughts. Not that it worked. She ought to have known that Hunter wouldn't settle for a platonic relationship. It had been a big mistake, agreeing to come out here.

She was the world's biggest fool; he had her exactly where he wanted her.

Agreeing to work for him, letting him cover her debts, had been extremely foolish. She should have known he would want his pound of flesh.

Her flesh.

Her body.

Here! Now!

Despite the warmth of the water her skin felt chilled, and she wrapped her arms about her and stood there miserably for several long minutes. Eventually, though, she pulled herself together and told herself that she was being childish.

She was woman enough, surely, not to let him manipulate her? If she didn't want him to kiss her, then she wouldn't let him. Whatever he wanted she would resist, with all the strength in her body.

Which could be pitifully weak where he was concerned, an inner voice reminded her.

But she stamped on it swiftly, and when she stepped out of the shower and pulled a huge fluffy towel around her shivering body she was determined that their relationship would remain entirely impersonal.

When she re-entered her bedroom she was shocked to see Hunter standing there, looking for all the world as though it was his right.

'What the hell are you doing here?' she demanded, clutching the towel tightly. 'Can't a girl have any privacy in this place?'

His hair was damp and curled close to his head, suggesting that he'd followed her lead and taken a shower himself. But why was he in her room? What did he want? What was he hoping for?

Her thoughts led to only one thing. And it made her realise how very vulnerable she was. Her eyes flickered towards the door as she wondered whether there was a lock, and to her relief she saw that there was. Next time she would remember to turn the key.

'You were a long time. I came to check that you were OK.'

'You could have knocked.'

'I did. I got no answer.'

'And so you thought you'd just come walking in?' she asked accusingly. 'How dare you? You might have some sort of hold over me until I've paid my debt but it doesn't include trespass. This is *my* room and I'd like you to respect that.' She hunched her shoulders and turned her back on him, hoping he would go.

But she didn't hear him move. In fact there was total silence. When she could stand it no longer she looked over her shoulder.

Hunter was still standing there. Smiling.

Damn the man! Keisha spun on her heel. 'Didn't you understand what I was saying?'

'Perfectly.'

'So why didn't you leave?'

'I wondered what you would do if I didn't?' And still he smiled.

Keisha fumed. 'If I were a man I'd throw you out,' she said tightly. 'But as I'm not I'm relying on your good manners to know when you're not wanted. Please go.'

'Of course—since you ask so nicely.'

His voice was filled with sarcasm, but to her surprise he spun round and headed for the door. Where he turned. 'I'll even go out for a while, Keisha. I'll give you that space you seem to so desperately want. But don't expect it to last for ever. I intend for us to have a close working relationship.'

And what else? she wondered. It was not until the door closed behind Hunter that she was able to relax. She threw herself down on the bed and stared at the ceiling. The white ceiling. Lord, it felt like a hospital in this place.

No, it didn't, she told herself quickly. She was just angry. It was beautiful and understated, and despite her misgivings she really did like it.

Finally she got dressed and wandered from room to room, admiring, finding it in her heart to be pleased for Hunter and all he had achieved. After she'd fully explored the house she went outside, surprised by the heat after the coolness indoors.

She explored the garden. The long curved pergola graced with bougainvillaea that afforded some relief from the scorching heat of the sun. The smooth sloping lawns that she guessed must be irrigated because they were lushly green. Beautiful flowering shrubs. And she found a tennis court as well as the swimming pool and a Jacuzzi.

There were paths that led to different gardens on different levels. It was intriguing and beautifully laid out—a riot of colour, in complete contrast to the interior of the house.

She enjoyed her afternoon exploring, and she enjoyed her freedom from Hunter, but in one way she was glad when he returned, because it was lonely on her own. His housekeeper was unfailingly polite, but she spoke little English and seemed to expect Keisha to amuse herself.

Keisha had imagined they would eat in the dining room, at the large table that would easily seat twelve, but instead their dinner was served out on the terrace. Under other circumstances it would have been a romantic setting, but Keisha was in no mood for romance, and the ambience of their surroundings failed to impress her. She was here under duress, and that was unlikely to change no matter how beautiful her environs, or how attentive Hunter was.

Nevertheless, the roast chicken served with a stew of green peppers, onions, tomatoes and courgettes, tempted her tastebuds.

'That was truly delicious,' she said. 'My compliments to your cook.'

She declined dessert, however. 'I couldn't eat another thing,' she admitted.

Afterwards they sat looking out to sea, neither talking, each alone with their thoughts. Until Hunter suddenly said, 'We'll go into Seville tomorrow, I'll show you my offices. And perhaps afterward we can explore the city.'

'If you insist,' she answered quietly. It was not something she would look forward to, in fact she couldn't think why he was suggesting it, but she knew that no amount of denial on her part would change his mind. 'It's been a long day,' she added. 'I think I'll go up to my room.'

'I'd like neither,' she answered quietly. It was not something she would look forward to, in fact she couldn't think why he was suggesting it, but she knew that no amount of denial on her part would change his mind.

'It's been a long day,' she added. 'I think I'll go up to my room.'

Before she could push herself up from her chair, however, his hand came down over hers. 'You're not running away like a scared rabbit. I'm not going to eat you, Keisha, despite what you might think. The night's still young. Why don't we stroll down to the beach?'

'No, thank you,' she said at once. 'I'm tired.'

'Tired? Or afraid?' An eyebrow rose and a note of impatience entered his voice.

Keisha tossed her head. 'Perhaps both. I also don't want to spend any more time in your company than is necessary.'

'Because?' he enquired.

Keisha wasn't sure how to answer. Because he disturbed her senses, was the real truth. Because she was beginning to get worried about the length of time they would be spending together. On a work basis she could handle it. But where leisure was concerned how could she ignore his profound sexuality? How could she avoid such close contact?

'Because,' she said finally, 'we have a history.'

'And that's a problem?'

'It's difficult to see you as someone I'm just working for.'

'You don't have to,' he said with a puzzled frown. 'We're more than that, surely? Ex-partners can still be friends. Close friends. It's what I'd like from you.'

'Friends and nothing else?' she asked, a determined glint in her eye.

'If it's what you want.'

'It is,' she declared strongly.

'On that basis, then,' he said, 'will you come down to the beach with me?'

'We can get there from here?' she asked, surprising herself by actually agreeing. She had to trust him some time, she supposed, or the whole situation would be sheer hell.

'It's quite a walk. I don't exactly have what you'd call a beachfront property. But it's well worth the effort.'

And so they made their way down a long curving track. Keisha was forced to look where she was walking, as tiny stones and pebbles made up part of their passage and she was afraid of slipping. The last thing she wanted was to feel Hunter's arms steadying her.

But they made their way safely down, and once on the shore Keisha kicked off her sandals and ran across the sand like a child on the first day of a holiday. The water was cool to her toes and she paddled happily, kicking the water, splashing through the shallows, forgetting for a moment that she was not alone.

To one side of them was a marina, filled with expensive boats, and to the other the hills rose steeply, studded with trees—probably olives, she thought—and red rooftops suggesting more dream-like villas nestling in their midst.

When Hunter's arms slid around her waist from behind she gave a tiny shriek. It was totally unexpected, and she tried to wriggle free. 'What are you doing?' she asked fiercely.

'You're difficult to resist—don't you know that?' His voice was low and suggestive, and sent all sorts of quivers through her limbs. 'And for once you looked totally relaxed.'

'Which I was, and now I'm not,' she slammed back at him. 'I thought I'd made it clear what sort of a relationship I want with you?' Goodness, was she out of her mind, responding so easily to this man? His very touch had sent all sorts of sensations reeling through her limbs. It was utter madness.

'It's a woman's prerogative to change her mind,' he reminded her.

'Not this woman,' she declared strongly, attempting to fight the conflicting emotions that threatened her sanity. Hunter had turned her to face him, and his eyes were hooded and intent upon hers, intent on reading her soul.

A shiver of fear ran through her.

'You're cold,' he said at once, and held her even more closely against him.

Keisha felt panic mounting, a deep, dark panic that both scared and excited her. She couldn't deny that the feel of

Hunter's body against hers was creating a storm, one that could break at any moment if she didn't free herself.

'Let me go,' she protested, her voice sounding loud and panic-stricken even to her own ears.

But Hunter had other ideas. 'You can't tell me that you're not feeling something? It's there in your eyes, in the heat of your skin, in that frantically beating pulse in your throat.'

Lord, why was he so observant? Keisha wondered whether she ought to sharply raise her knee—or give in to temptation…

When Hunter's lips claimed hers the decision was made for her. This was so wrong, so very wrong. She twisted her head from side to side. 'This is not what I want,' she hissed. 'Keep away from me.'

'You would deny your own needs?' he asked, with a smile in his voice.

'Why would I need you?' she snapped. 'You made my life hell once. I'm not going to let you do it again.'

Hunter backed off, his eyes growing suddenly cold. 'Hell? Is that what it was? Is that what it felt like?'

Keisha realised that perhaps she'd gone too far, but she was not going to back down. 'Some of the time.' She jutted her chin. 'You have no idea.'

'It seems not,' he admitted bitterly. 'And is it hell with me here now?'

Keisha closed her eyes for a few seconds. 'I've hardly had time to find out.'

'I don't want it to be hell,' he announced gruffly. 'I want you to enjoy yourself. I want you to—like me a little.'

Heavens, she liked him more than a little. Already old emotions were revived. If she was afraid of anyone it was herself—of the feelings that had begun to run rampant inside her.

His hands touched her shoulders and he looked deep into her eyes, and when she made no attempt to pull away he gathered her to him once again. 'My sweet Keisha, you have nothing to fear.'

The powerful blue of his eyes instantly captured her. And this time when his lips touched hers, gently at first, experimentally, and then, finding no resistance, becoming more persuasive, Keisha discovered to her dismay that she didn't want him to stop.

She allowed her lips to part and let him kiss her with a passion that reminded her of the early days of their marriage, so that almost without thinking she kissed him back, urging her body close to his, feeling his need of her, feeling excited by it.

It was, of course, their surroundings that was doing this to her, she told herself. It was this lovely part of the world, so different from central London—a city that never slept, with its many thousands of buildings that hid the gorgeous sunsets, beautiful though most of them were.

Here was the Mediterranean and the huge sky, a big wide-open space that both encouraged and embraced. Already the sun had begun its slow descent, and was weaving its spell.

She closed her eyes. Best not to look, not to feel, not to relate. But then Hunter kissed her eyelids, each one in turn with gentle butterfly kisses. And her nose. And her ears. And finally her mouth again.

There was no denying that he was a fantastic kisser. Her bones had melted. If he let her go she would fall into a heap at his feet; she would dissolve in the water that still lapped at their ankles.

Her breathing grew deeper, and when finally Hunter lifted his head, when he looked at her with slumberous eyes, asking a silent question, she could only smile.

'I think we should go back to the villa,' he said softly.

Back to his room, he meant.

What heaven that would be! But common sense prevailed. The climb would give her time to push this whole event to the back of her mind, to warn herself never to let it happen again.

It proved how easily she could succumb. It proved what a master he was in the art of seduction. Or had she been seduced by their surroundings, not by this big man himself?

Perhaps Hunter had known all along what this beautiful part of the Spanish coast would do to her? He had counted on it!

And she had not let him down!

During the long haul back up to his villa, Keisha berated herself for showing him that he still had the power to arouse her senses. And she tried to keep as much distance between them as possible. Which was difficult when the loose surface made her constantly lose her footing.

More than once his steadying hand saved her, but on the final stretch, when she slipped particularly badly, he was not quick enough. Keisha winced as she felt the gravel graze her knees and palms, and she felt extremely foolish when he helped her up.

'Are you hurt?' His concern was genuine.

'A little, I think,' she admitted, looking down at her legs and lifting her hands for his inspection.

'It's my fault for not watching you more closely,' he said, his voice harsh with self-recrimination.

'Nonsense,' retorted Keisha. 'It's a dangerous path; it could happen to anyone.'

'Especially when they're wearing ridiculous sandals.'

Keisha could hear the sudden smile in his voice, and she

looked at him and he was laughing. She looked down at her feet in her pretty but impractical mules. 'I guess I should have changed them.'

'I guess you should. I'd best carry you the rest of the way.' And before Keisha could protest he had swung her up into his arms.

They were almost at the top anyway. Keisha wondered whether he would have been so gallant if he'd had to carry her all the way. She could feel the strong beat of his heart, smell the sexy male scent of him, and although she wanted to yell at him to put her down, it was really rather a nice feeling.

Once they were on level ground, however, she wriggled out of his grasp. 'Thank you. I'll go and clean myself up now.' And she ran towards the house.

But if she thought she was going to get away from him for the rest of the evening she was mistaken. Hunter followed her into her room. 'Let me do it,' he said gently. 'Sit there and I'll bring a first aid kit.'

Realising it would be churlish to refuse, Keisha waited. Hunter bathed her knees and her palms, checked to make sure nothing was embedded, and then, to her dismay and despite her protests, he bandaged them thoroughly.

When he was finished he gave a satisfied smile.

'What am I supposed to do now?' she queried frantically, holding her hands out and looking at them as though they didn't belong to her.

'You have no choice but to let me look after you,' he claimed, and she felt sure that there was a note of triumph in his voice.

'This is ridiculous,' she cried, and began to tear off the bandages. But Hunter closed in on her, taking her hands into his, effectively making her his prisoner. And then he kissed her again, and Keisha knew that if she didn't stand her ground now they would end up in bed.

But she hadn't taken into account Hunter's determination. 'Looking after you, my sweet,' he said, lifting his mouth fractionally from hers, 'could never be counted as ridiculous. It is my duty—and my pleasure.' And, as if to confirm how much pleasure, he claimed her lips again.

Keisha felt both fear and enjoyment. Fear that things could go too far, and enjoyment in the taste of Hunter's kisses. He was truly a magical man. He could make her do whatever he wanted. Her wishes were ignored—both by him and herself.

She was putty in his hands. His kisses awoke passions she would far rather have lain dormant. In fact she had thought they were dead—until Hunter came back into her life!

How foolish was that?

How could one man do this to her?

When that man was Hunter it was easily explained. She would have to be inhuman not to react to him.

Her heart thumped fit to burst, and the blood pumped through her body at twice its normal speed. She wanted to yell at him; she wanted to tell him to leave her alone, to get out. But her throat was so constricted by desire that it would let no sound out.

Except perhaps a low groan of pleasure.

Hunter heard, and his kisses grew more invasive, drawing from her a feverish response. He freed her hands and urged her towards the bed, and instead of resisting Keisha let the thrill of the moment take over.

In her mind she knew that later she would regret it, but for the moment she was powerless. It was as though the years in between had never happened. They were husband and wife again.

Her body belonged to Hunter!

Hunter felt his heart trying to leap out of his chest, felt a re-kindling of the passion that had died when he saw Keisha with another man. Then he dismissed it. No, no, *no!* He mustn't feel anything. This wasn't passion; this was revenge. He was about to use her body. He would find no pleasure in it. He was simply punishing her for daring to walk out on him. Showing her what pleasures could still have been hers.

She would never know the torment she had put him through—how devastated he'd been when she'd left him for someone else. It was as though his heart had been torn out. He had thought he would never get over it. In fact he hadn't. For three years it had simmered at the back of his mind.

Seeing her again at the party had brought back with a vengeance all the anger he had experienced, and the disappointment, the fear that she might never have truly loved him, had simply married him for the lifestyle he could give her.

Even then she hadn't been satisfied, he thought bitterly. She really did deserve to be hurt as much as she had hurt him. Revenge was going to be very sweet indeed.

As he stripped off his clothes with impatient hands he asked himself whether he was rushing things. This was their first night here. He hadn't intended to move in on her quite so quickly. He didn't want to frighten her away before he'd even begun.

But neither had he expected that Keisha would give herself up so easily.

She lay there on the bed, watching him. She looked so innocent. So defenceless!

And he was a swine for taking advantage.

With an angry shake of his head Hunter snatched up his clothes and stormed out of the room. He couldn't do it. Not yet. Not with Keisha looking at him with those trusting green eyes.

Yes, he wanted to make love to her, and he wanted her to fall in love with him again, quite desperately, but being intimate now was not the way to do it. She was at a low ebb because of her fall. She was shaken up. In the morning she would come to her senses and would hate him for it—even more than she already did!

And getting her on side would be harder than ever.

Keisha felt bereft. She knew that Hunter had wanted to make love to her, so why had he walked out? An attack of conscience? Somehow she couldn't believe that. It had to be something more.

Actually she ought to be thankful; instead she felt strangely violated. With his wicked blue eyes and fantastically sexy mouth he had aroused in her feelings that were best left alone. Feelings that should have remained buried for evermore. So why weren't they?

Cursing silently, Keisha rolled over with her back to the door, curling into a foetal position and closing her eyes tightly. And like that she went to sleep. She wasn't aware of Hunter quietly opening the door some time later, tiptoeing across the room and covering her over. She wasn't aware that he stood there for several minutes with a curiously satisfied smile on his face.

What she did know was that she awoke to find it dark and that she was still fully dressed. Drowsily she slipped out of her skirt and top and crawled back beneath the covers. She knew nothing else until morning.

This was the day they were going to Seville, remembered Keisha unhappily as she showered. Another whole day spent in Hunter's company. He had so very nearly climbed into bed with her yesterday that she couldn't help but wonder how today would end.

She would need to be on her guard—at all times!

She dressed in a pair of white shorts and a pretty lemon top, and when she joined Hunter on the terrace she fixed a purpose-built smile on her face. 'Good morning!' she said brightly.

Hunter looked up from the newspaper he was reading—a Spanish one, she noticed—and smiled also. 'Good morning, Keisha. How are the injuries this morning?'

'Completely better.' She held out her hands for his inspection, having removed the bandages earlier.

'Good!' He looked pleased. 'So it won't curtail our outing?'

'Not at all,' she answered. 'I'm looking forward to it.' In an odd sort of way. At least out of the house she wouldn't feel so suffocated by his presence.

After breakfast Hunter led her out to his car—a beautiful silver Aston Martin convertible.

'We're going in this?' she asked breathlessly.

'Sure thing,' he answered. 'It's my new baby. Do you like it?'

'It's beautiful,' she breathed. She ran her hand over the polished metal and admired its sleek lines.

'Jump in, then,' he encouraged.

Keisha almost wished she hadn't agreed. It was distinctly cosy in this classy little sports car, with hardly enough room to breathe, and certainly nowhere to go. She was penned in beside Hunter whether she liked it or not.

'Hold on to your hat,' he said as he opened the throttle, and they almost hurtled through the lanes until they reached the highway, where he opened it up even more.

Finally she settled down and enjoyed the journey.

The countryside was mountainous and breathtaking, though in point of fact she was more aware of Hunter than anything around her. They drove through miles of olive groves and acres of cereal farms before they finally reached Seville.

'Legend has it,' Hunter informed her as they stretched their legs in his office car park, 'that Seville was founded by Hercules.'

Keisha lifted her brows but didn't remark on it.

They spent over an hour at his place of work. Many pairs of eyes were cast curiously in Keisha's direction, and she felt most uncomfortable. Nevertheless she was impressed with the set-up. They were modern offices, in a brand-new marble building, and it looked as though no expense had been spared.

And every female there was in love with Hunter. It amused Keisha to see the way their eyes followed him, the way they whispered behind his back, the way their eyes fluttered and their cheeks coloured when he spoke to them.

Business over, Hunter took her out to lunch in one of Seville's finest restaurants, and after that they explored the city. Keisha surprised herself by enjoying the day. Hunter showed off his knowledge of Seville's history, and Keisha found it most sensual and romantic. She would certainly like to explore in more depth at some other time.

Preferably on her own.

Or at least not with someone as sexy as Hunter. He treated her as though she were very special to him, taking her hand, smiling down into her face, even hugging her to him. It was like going out on a first date all over again.

And every time he showered her with attention Keisha felt a surge of emotion and the memory of far happier days, when she would have eagerly lifted her face for his kiss. And it somehow saddened her that Hunter made no attempt to kiss her now.

Which was stupid. Because she knew where his kisses could lead.

As she found out when they got back to his villa!

CHAPTER EIGHT

HUNTER KNEW THAT he almost had Keisha where he wanted her, and tonight he intended that she sleep in his bed. Tonight would be the beginning of the end for this very special lady.

The day had gone much better than he expected. Keisha had been receptive, interested in everything around her, and she hadn't even objected when he took her to the office. Not that he'd introduced her to anyone except by her Christian name. He'd let her be the mystery lady.

No one knew that he'd once been married, as far as they were concerned he was an extremely eligible bachelor, and he was well aware that everyone wondered why some very glamorous female had never snapped him up. There were plenty of contenders, that was for sure, but he was interested in no one.

Keisha had been the love of his life, and she had killed that love. Maybe he'd been guilty to a certain extent of neglecting her, but surely not so much that she'd needed the company of other men? They'd still had a good love-life, despite the long hours he'd worked. He could never forgive her for walking out. She deserved whatever she had coming to her.

They ate a light supper and then sat outside, enjoying the

evening sunshine, and for a while neither of them spoke. 'What are you thinking?' he asked eventually.

Keisha turned to look at him with those wide green eyes of hers—eyes that had once excited every inch of him! 'How much I've enjoyed today,' she answered.

And amazingly they could still excite! He could already feel a stirring in his groin—which he tried to ignore. This wasn't part of the exercise. 'What did you like best?'

'All of it,' answered Keisha. 'But mainly I think the cathedral, because it's so vast and so richly decorated, and the Tower of Gold, because of its history and the fact that it's all that remains of Seville's medieval fortifications.'

Hunter's brows rose a little. 'I'm impressed. I didn't realise that you had a fancy for old buildings.'

Keisha shrugged. 'I guess there's a lot about me you don't know.'

'Because I wasn't a good enough husband and you ran out on me?' he snorted through flared nostrils. Damn! He hadn't intended to get angry. They'd had such a companionable day—more than that, actually. They'd been very close, and he'd wanted to carry it on to its ultimate conclusion.

He smiled with difficulty. 'I'm sorry; I shouldn't have said that. I enjoyed today too.' Which he had—very much—more than he'd expected. He'd enjoyed showing Keisha the sights, watching her face, seeing her wonderment, his appreciation, joy, even. Yes, it had been a good day.

And the night was going to be even better!

'More wine?' he asked. He'd brought the remains of a bottle out with him, and he leaned forward now, bottle in hand, ready to pour her another glass.

But Keisha shook her head. 'Any more and I'll have a headache.'

Meaning she'd retire to her room early, before he could seduce her. Immediately he put the bottle back down and inched his chair closer to hers.

'I'm glad you appreciate the beauty of this part of the world,' he said softly. 'It means a lot to me. My mother was half-Spanish; did you know that? I feel closer to her here.'

'No, I didn't know,' answered Keisha.

Her smile was warm and she was totally relaxed. He could smell her perfume and feel her sensuality. She had changed into a low-cut pink dress with frills at the shoulders and a flared knee-length skirt. It suited her beautifully, and she looked sexy and gorgeous, but what he really wanted to do was rip it off. He wanted to ravage her body and make her his—once again!

It was hard being patient.

He reached out and took her hand. 'Thank you for your company today.' And then he lifted it and pressed a kiss into her palm, closing her fingers over it, and all the time he never took his eyes off hers.

And amazingly, as though she couldn't help herself, she leaned closer towards him. 'You don't have to thank me,' she whispered. 'It's I who should be thanking you for taking me. Seville is a magical city.'

'But not as magical as you,' he growled softly in response. 'You're so beautiful—do you realise that?' And with his eyes locked into hers, praying she wouldn't back off, he closed the gap between them and allowed his lips to lightly brush hers.

Nothing more—just a feather light touch. Then he withdrew and waited. And when she didn't move, when her lustrous eyes didn't stray for one second, he kissed her again. This time he maintained the contact.

He felt the stirrings of a response in her lips, and with a

groan that he couldn't contain he hooked his hand behind her head. She tasted sweeter than he'd ever remembered—and there were lots of memories. Her lips were soft and pliant under his…so willing!

But patience was the name of the game here. He exulted in her sense of urgency; she was playing right into his hands. And he smiled deep down inside, at the same time trying to ignore the fact that he too felt a manic need. A hunger deep in his groin that demanded immediate release.

Still with his mouth on hers, he got to his feet, letting one hand slide beneath her shoulders, hooking the other beneath her knees. He lifted her up and carried her to the settee, where he continued to kiss her, deepening it, fuelling the urgency inside him, feeling a similar response from Keisha.

It was no wonder he had never been able to get her out of his head, much as he'd tried to do so. His one big aim, after he had bumped into her again, had been to destroy her as she had destroyed him—*and this was why!* Because she had denied him the greatest pleasure life could offer. Because she had withdrawn her body from his. Because she had declared that she no longer wanted to be his wife.

How cruel was that?

His grip on Keisha tightened so much that she cried out. Immediately he regained control of himself. Heavens, he would need to be careful. Kissing her gently again now, nibbling her ear, murmuring words that meant nothing at all, he exulted in the excitement he could feel rising in her body.

Her breathing had quickened, but so too had his. Her eyes were closed; her head was lolling back. He ran a finger down her throat, feeling the madly beating pulse, and then slid his fingers beneath the low-cut dress to feel the smooth swell of her breasts.

His testosterone levels shot sky-high, swift heat invaded his body, and his heart hammered so hard that he felt sure she must hear. He ran an urgent thumb over her nipple and felt it leap into immediate response. Oh, Lord, how he wanted to take it into his mouth, to suckle her breast, to feed from her as he had so many times in the past.

She tasted good, he knew that, and he wanted to taste her again; he wanted to make her his in every way possible. He couldn't wait; he couldn't do this thing slowly, as he'd planned.

'Keisha!' His voice was low and guttural as his head bowed to her breast, and when Keisha's hands clasped his head, holding him there, showing him how much she wanted this too, he could feel himself losing control.

With one swift movement he swung her up into his arms again and without a word carried her into the house. He almost ran up the stairs and, kicking open the door to his room, he laid her down on the bed.

She stared at him, her eyes wide and soft and particularly brilliant. Were they begging him to make love to her or were they imploring him to stop? He couldn't quite make it out. The fact that she didn't speak, that she simply lay there with her lips parted and her breast heaving, made him suspect that she needed him as much as he needed her.

If that were possible.

With shaking hands he tore off his shirt, wrenched down the zip on his trousers and dragged them off, followed swiftly by his socks and lastly his boxers. And all the time he never took his eyes from hers.

It delighted him when Keisha wriggled out of her dress with the same indecent haste, when she snapped her tiny lacy bra undone and discarded it with her equally minuscule briefs.

Slender as she was, her figure was deliciously tantalising, and he lay down beside her, wanting to feast his eyes, wanting to touch, to trail, to enjoy her body slowly and seductively.

But how impossible was that?

Keisha too couldn't wait. Their mouths and tongues touched and joined and explored; their hands did the same. She was his for the taking!

As he was hers! This definitely hadn't been part of his plan; he wasn't supposed to get emotionally involved. But he was, and there was nothing he could do about it except take and enjoy.

Even as he was thinking about it Keisha lay back and opened her arms to him. With their eyes locked together he lowered himself over her, taking her gently at first, but then, urged on by her cries, by her bucking, hungry body, he thrust himself deeply inside her.

He would have liked the experience to last—but how could it when they were both so ready, both so hungry, both so much in need? His whole body pulsed frenziedly and he lost control, his world exploded, and seconds later he felt Keisha writhing beneath him, experiencing the same mind-blowing pleasure.

He rolled onto his side and they held each other for long pleasure-filled minutes. Until their bodies returned to normal, until sanity overtook them and they suddenly realised what they had done.

At least Keisha did. She looked horrified.

Whereas he, deep down inside, where Keisha couldn't see, was exultant.

The battle plan had begun.

Spectacularly!

* * *

Keisha could not believe how foolish she had been. She had let Hunter see how easily he could seduce her. How idiotic was that?

The trouble was he was so utterly, utterly gorgeous. The sexiest man on the planet! And she had given him up, she reminded herself. She'd had no business letting him touch her again. It was fatal. No woman in her right mind could resist him—not when he set himself out to charm.

Which he had this evening.

Why? she wondered. What was he trying to prove? That he was still irresistible to her? If that was the case he had well and truly succeeded. What must he be thinking? That she still had feelings for him. That he could use her now whenever he liked?

Afraid to look him in the eye, Keisha rolled over and scrambled off the bed. With her clothes tucked beneath her arm she fled across the room. But she didn't get far.

'Keisha!' Hunter's voice halted her hurried steps. 'I thought it was what you wanted. Don't run away from me now.'

'I thought it was too,' she said, turning but not quite able to face him. 'Until I realised what I was doing. I'm not here for this, Hunter. I'm here to work. I don't want an affair with you.'

'That's a pity,' he murmured, 'because I'd very much like an affair with you.'

'It's not going to happen, Hunter,' she told him quietly. 'Tonight was a mistake—one that I'm not likely to repeat.'

'But you did enjoy it?'

She nodded, embarrassed to admit it—but what else could she do?

'So what's the problem? Why shouldn't we have a bit of fun while we're out here?'

'Fun? Is that what you call it?' she asked hotly. 'I call it a personal attack on my defences. Let me tell you this, Hunter: from now on I shall be on my guard at all times. There will be no more sneaking up on me. Do you understand that?'

'Is that what I did? Sneak up?' he asked, a smile tugging at the corners of his lips.

'As good as!' she snapped.

'I thought you knew exactly what I was doing.'

Actually she had, and she'd been unable to stop him. But she wasn't going to tell him that. 'You took advantage,' she accused.

'Of what, precisely?'

Keisha wasn't sure how to answer that. She'd been as eager as he to make love, and he knew it. 'You seduced me. All day long.'

His smile widened. 'And here was I thinking how nice it was to have you relax in my company instead of being your enemy number one. How mistaken can a guy get?'

Keisha knew that he was teasing her, and she whipped around and stormed off to her room. But Hunter hadn't given up. He followed, pushing the door open before she could lock it. 'So what's really troubling you, Keisha?'

She looked at him boldly. 'You're surely not thinking that you can persuade me to move back in with you on a permanent basis? That's not in your mind, is it?'

'Why would I do that?' he asked.

Keisha frowned, her eyes full of suspicion. He sounded too innocent. 'Because there's something about you that I can't fathom. You're being too nice to me. I'm the wife who ran out on you—have you forgotten? I'm the person who got herself so badly into debt that you had to help out. Why would you be nice to me?'

Hunter spread his hand expansively, still smiling. 'Because I'm a nice guy! Will that do?

Keisha shook her head in desperation. 'OK, Mr Nice Guy, if you're that nice get out of my room.'

To her amazement he did as she asked—except that he turned in the doorway and blew her a kiss. 'Until tomorrow, my beautiful, passionate Keisha.'

Keisha sank down on the edge of the bed, hating herself, hating Hunter, and hating everything about this place. What had she done?

She had opened the door for Hunter to move in on her whenever he felt like it, that was what.

Letting him make love to her had been a big mistake. One she would regret for the rest of her life. What she must do now was make sure it never happened again.

But how easy would that be? He had made her realise that she was no longer immune to him. How could she possibly live in the same house for six whole months? Denying herself the pleasures he could create within her would be sheer purgatory.

Maybe she ought to fly home now, before anything else happened? Except that that would be running away again. She needed to stand up to her fears. Surely she was woman enough?

At eighteen she had barely been capable of making up her own mind. She had let her heart rule her head. But not now. Not ever again. Especially after her earlier performance!

With a savage twist of her mouth she got up and headed for the shower, and beneath the stinging hot water she scrubbed Hunter off her skin and out of her mind.

Wrapping a thin cotton robe about her, she sat on her balcony watching the sky darken and fill with a curtain of stars. Had it been any other time she would have marvelled at its beauty, but not tonight.

Tonight she was angry with herself. She had no time for anything magical or heart-stopping. She had fallen at the first hurdle. Now she must make sure it never happened again. And the only way she could do that was to harden her heart against Hunter.

Keisha slept little that night, but by morning she knew the road she must take. She was Hunter's personal assistant. Nothing more. She dressed in a severe white blouse and a straight skirt, and when she presented herself at breakfast she almost smiled at the look of shock on Hunter's face.

'What's this?' he asked frowningly.

'My office uniform,' she retorted. 'Is there any coffee, Mr Donahue?'

'Mr Donahue be damned!' he roared. 'Even Alison called me Hunter when we were alone. If this is some trick of yours to—'

'It's no trick,' cut in Keisha sharply. 'I'm here to work— isn't that right? I'd be obliged if you'd join me in the office after breakfast. I want nothing more than coffee myself. I'll take it upstairs.'

She almost smiled when she saw Hunter's astonished face. Clearly he had never expected such an outburst from her.

And then his face relaxed. 'This is a joke, yes?'

'Not at all. I'm perfectly serious.'

'I insist you join me for breakfast. You cannot work on an empty stomach.'

'I can and I will,' she replied, and headed out of the room.

But Hunter caught her wrist and yanked her down on a chair. 'I said you will join me.'

Keisha bit back a harsh retort. If they had to work together they at least needed to be civil, and angering him now was not the way to go about it. But if he dared to try anything on…

He poured her coffee and pushed a basket of toasted rolls in her direction. 'Help yourself.'

Keisha glared, thought about refusing, then decided against it. She took a roll, broke it in two, ignored the olive oil that Hunter favoured, and spread it with butter and preserve instead. It tasted like sawdust. But she swallowed it nevertheless, conscious that Hunter was watching her closely.

'Why,' he asked, when she had finished, 'have you become a chameleon?'

Keisha frowned. 'I don't know what you mean.'

'Don't you?' His eyes narrowed in a steady stare. 'Maybe you don't change colour but you certainly change your way of thinking.'

'Yesterday was a mistake,' she snapped.

'A mistake, eh?' One eyebrow rose. 'And you're telling me that it isn't one you'd care to repeat?'

'Not ever!' she thrust. 'Didn't I make myself clear last night?'

'Oh, very. But I thought that perhaps after a night's sleep you might—'

'Change my mind? Not a cat in hell's chance, *Mr* Donahue.'

His lips tightened until they almost disappeared, and his blue eyes turned as dark as a midnight sky.

Keisha thought she heard him swear under his breath, but she couldn't be sure. All she knew was that she must not let him see by the merest chink in her armour that he still had the power to arouse her like no one else ever could.

'Then I guess it's down to business,' he snarled, and preceded her out of the room.

Keisha couldn't help wondering what sort of a can of worms she had opened. Life was definitely not going to be easy. She had known that from the start. But she hadn't realised exactly how much temptation would be put her way, or how hard it would be to deny herself the pleasure of Hunter's body.

However, for the rest of the day he kept her so busy that she didn't have time to think about their relationship. He was brusque and efficient, and expected her to do everything in record time.

He spoke fluent Spanish—which she supposed he had learned from his mother—but mostly he liaised with his London office, for which she was thankful. She had been taught French at school, but her Spanish was limited to a few useful holiday phrases.

After work, when they'd shut down the computers and closed the office, he changed again. He became once more the man she had married, charming and attentive—and a complete danger to her psyche.

'How about a swim before supper?' he suggested.

Keisha nodded. It sounded like an excellent idea. A few lengths would relieve the tension that had built up during the day—and maybe, just maybe, she'd be able to steer clear of him.

It was wishful thinking. Hunter didn't actually touch her, but he swam around her, he swam under her and over her like a playful porpoise, and she didn't have to be Einstein to guess that it was a sort of foreplay and that his intention was to make love to her.

No matter how much she told herself that she was being foolish, that she would deeply regret any involvement with

Hunter, Keisha found herself falling under his spell. Her hormones were dancing all over the place, and for just a brief moment she wondered whether it would be feasible to have a six-month affair with him and then walk away.

How stupid was that? It would be humanly impossible. Last night had taught her how easily she could succumb when he set out to charm. In fact she was beginning to wonder whether she had ever stopped loving him.

Her trouble was that she didn't know what Hunter wanted. What sort of game he was playing. Was he using her? Was he teaching her a lesson, showing her what she was missing? Would he turn his back on her at the end of it all?

It was not a pleasant thought.

Or maybe she was doing him an injustice? Maybe he genuinely wanted her back in his life? It could be the reason he had never remarried.

She would have liked to think that that was the case, but somehow she doubted it. He said he'd tried to find her, but he couldn't have tried very hard. Someone would have told him. Even her mother might have broken eventually, if he'd been persistent enough.

No, he was using her.

And she, fool that she was, was letting him.

The trouble was she couldn't resist. No matter how often she told herself that she was being unwise her body let her down. Even now her blood sizzled through her veins. He was so totally, devastatingly magnificent that—

Her thoughts were interrupted by firm hands around her waist. She was plucked from the water and set down on the side of the pool. In seconds Hunter had hauled himself out and pulled her to her feet. And in less than another second she felt herself crushed against his cool throbbing body.

There was no denying what he wanted—what she wanted too! But it wouldn't be wise. Not again. It would give him the wrong idea. He would think that she was his for the taking whenever he felt like it.

He let her go, and she watched as he took the padded cushions off one or two of the chairs dotted around the pool and flung them on the floor. His eyes were almost coal black as he faced her again.

'I can't, Hunter,' she said quietly, as he began stripping off his trunks.

He frowned, stopping his frenzied movements. 'What do you mean, can't? You want this as much as I do.'

'Perhaps,' she admitted. 'But it's all wrong. We're divorced; I'm here to work. It's not right that we—'

'Not right be damned,' he swore. 'You didn't say that last night.'

'It was a mistake,' she declared. 'I've already told you that.' But oh, Lord, she really did want him to make love to her.

Passion flared in his eyes. 'I think you protest too much.' Hunter said softly, and got down to Keisha's level. Without breaking eye contact he slowly began to remove her swimsuit. He then began to kiss her gently on the lips, tentatively at first, and then gradually working his way down her body with more intensity. Thrilled at the senses his kisses stirred in her body, Keisha resigned herself to the fact that this was what she wanted. Only this. Only Hunter.

It had always been like this between them. Swift and pleasurable. No sooner had their bodies grown feverish with desire than they had made love. Hot, passionate love. Obviously there had been times when they took things more slowly, but that first overheated hunger had always taken preference. The more languid lovemaking had come later.

This was hot and passionate. Hunter made love to her as though he had never done so before. And Keisha couldn't control herself either. All thoughts of resisting him were forgotten. They were both lost in a spiralling world of senses which spun them out into orbit and then brought them crashing back.

It lasted no more than a few minutes. But it had been, thought Keisha, more exciting than ever before. Hunter's lovemaking seemed to get better. She had never thought it possible. Whether or not it was a case of absence heightening her feelings she didn't know, but as she lay there fighting for breath she felt sad that it was over so quickly.

Hunter pushed himself up on one elbow and looked at her. 'Are you going to tell me off again?'

Keisha shook her head, wanting to, desperately. But she couldn't. 'There's not much point, is there?' Her voice was no more than a husky, trembling whisper.

'My beautiful Keisha.' Hunter pulled her against him. 'Why did we ever part when we're so clearly made for one another?'

Keisha murmured something unintelligible. She didn't want to bring up her reason for running away—not while their bodies still throbbed, not while they were so close and so comfortable in each other's presence.

If only it had always been like this. If only Hunter hadn't insisted on working such long hours. Perhaps he wouldn't now that he'd become a success? Perhaps he was a changed man? Perhaps she ought to give him another chance?

Or was this her heart talking and not her head?

It could be that he didn't want another chance; he was just enjoying her body.

This thought had Keisha rolling away from him and

jumping to her feet. 'We can't lie here for ever,' she said, by way of an excuse. 'Someone might see us.'

'And who might that someone be?' he asked softly. 'You're running scared, aren't you, my sweet? You're still afraid of your own emotions! Don't be! They're beautiful and precious and I want you to share them with me.'

Keisha closed her eyes. Heaven help her, it was what she wanted too.

CHAPTER NINE

HUNTER WAS PLEASED with the way Keisha was falling so very nicely into his trap. He naturally still needed to tread carefully—he mustn't let his enthusiasm run away with him—but if their last two lovemaking sessions were anything to go by it wouldn't be too long before he was in a position to exact his revenge.

Surprisingly, the path to her destruction was more pleasurable than he had imagined. So swift had been her capitulation that he'd even begun to wonder whether she had ever really fallen out of love with him.

No! He mustn't think that—not even for one second. She wouldn't have left him if she still loved him. She'd left him for someone else! Because the grass had been greener on the other side!

Even now his blood boiled when he thought about the day he'd returned home and she'd gone. He'd felt shell-shocked. He'd walked around the house in a blaze of anger and disbelief. He'd nearly gone out of his mind. And when he'd later seen her in someone else's arms it had nearly tipped the scales.

One day he would ask her about that other guy, but he would bide his time. It wasn't now. He didn't want to say anything that would antagonise her. But the truth would come out, of that he was very sure, and her destruction would be complete.

It was small compensation that Marc Collins, if that was who it was, hadn't proved to be Mr Right either. Perhaps Keisha would never find her perfect man. But in the meantime he would do—was that what she was thinking?

Hunter tensed every muscle in his body, if she was using him! If she were pursuing his body but nothing else, then his plan would backfire badly.

He couldn't afford to take the risk that she was the one calling the tune. He had to *make* her fall for him.

Keisha realised that she needed to be very careful where Hunter was concerned. He was taking advantage of their situation. And she, silly idiot that she was, found it difficult to resist him. Actually, she was in grave danger of giving too much of herself.

And she mustn't do that. It would be fatal. She still had feelings of guilt about not telling him of her miscarriage. It wouldn't have mattered so much if they weren't getting so close—but they were. And the closer they got the more pressure she would feel to tell him.

In actual fact she owed it to him.

But how could she? After all these years? He would explode. Her life wouldn't be worth living. No, she must wait—at least until she had repaid her debt. She hated owing him money. Although he had said it didn't matter, her own integrity wouldn't let her accept his more than generous offer.

Then one morning she had a call from her friend, Gillian.

'Keisha, I'm in Spain. I'm holidaying with Erica and Joanne. Can I come and see you tomorrow?'

'Of course.' Keisha was highly delighted. She missed her friend—she missed someone to talk to, someone to confide in. 'Whereabouts are you? I'll ask Hunter to send a car.'

'Send a car indeed! Listen to you!' declared Gillian. 'Haven't we gone up in the world? But I won't say no. I'm in Marbella.'

When Keisha told Hunter he was instantly agreeable. 'It will be good for you to have some female company. How long's she coming for?'

'I don't know,' answered Keisha. 'Just for the day, I imagine.'

When Gillian arrived the next morning Hunter announced that he was going out. 'I'll leave you to your girlie talk,' he said. 'Have fun!'

'This is an amazing place,' declared Gillian after he'd gone. 'Come and give me a guided tour.' Gillian was tall and slender, with flaming red hair and an outgoing personality, and was pretty in an unconventional sort of way.

With each room they went into she was duly impressed. 'But white?' she asked. 'I mean he's *all* man, isn't he?' There was admiration in her eyes. 'I imagined him to prefer strong colours.'

Keisha shrugged. 'He left it to his designer.'

'Ah!' exclaimed Gillian, smiling. 'He was besotted with her, yes? Didn't want to say no to anything? Mmm! I wonder if he paid her in kind?'

'Gillian!' scolded Keisha, but secretly she had wondered the same thing. The villa was elegant and beautiful, but it wasn't Hunter. Although, having initially thought that, she had grown used to it, and had to admit that it was calming and soothing—and it wasn't entirely white everywhere; there were splashes of colour that you didn't notice at first. It was very cleverly done.

She showed her friend all of the rooms except Hunter's bedroom, deciding that it was too private for her friend's prying eyes.

But Gillian had no such qualms. 'This is Hunter's room, I presume?' she said, pushing open the only remaining door. And before Keisha could stop her she walked in.

'Hunter, you disappoint me,' were her first words. 'On the other hand!' she exclaimed when she entered his bathroom and saw the stunning round bath. 'This is to die for! I bet you've had some good times in here?'

To her dismay Keisha blushed. 'Let's go and look around outside,' she suggested quickly, ignoring her friend's question.

Gillian lifted knowing brows, but for the moment said nothing more. Later, though, sitting on the terrace enjoying iced tea and the terrific views over the Mediterranean, she brought the subject up again. 'So what's going on between you and Hunter? Are you getting back together?'

Keisha pulled a face. 'No—definitely not! Although we have made love,' she confessed. There was no way she could commit to him entirely—not with her guilty secret still hanging over her head. And would she ever find the strength to confess?

'Sex was always good between you two. I know it was. You always had this wonderful glow about you. I was so envious. I've never met a guy who made me look like that.' Gillian sighed, and was silent for a few moments before saying, 'It's so beautiful out here—such a gorgeous villa, such a gorgeous setting—no wonder you've been seduced into climbing into bed with him. Given half a chance I'd do it myself.'

'Gillian!' exclaimed Keisha.

Her friend shrugged. 'I've always fancied him, as you very

well know. Not that I ever got a look in with you around. He adores you, Keisha.'

'He might have done once,' said Keisha quickly. 'But don't forget he ruined our marriage. He put work before me. He didn't even try very hard to find me when I ran away. Doesn't that tell you something?' She didn't mention her suspicions about his affair. She'd never told Gillian that she'd thought he was seeing someone else. She found it far too embarrassing to admit that her man had been so dissatisfied with her that he'd sought pleasure elsewhere.

'So there's no chance of a reconciliation?'

Keisha shook her head firmly. 'None at all!' As far as she was concerned Hunter was exploiting the situation. Not that she didn't enjoy their lovemaking. She did. It was fantastic. But this period of time was nothing more than an interlude. It might even be their surroundings that moved her, that made her respond to Hunter in a way she had never expected or wanted to do again.

'So why are you—intimate with him?' It was Gillian's turn to frown this time. 'Aren't you heading for trouble?'

'Maybe,' she admitted, with a lift of her thin shoulders. 'But sometimes I can't help myself. He's too persuasive by far.'

'Do you think he's using you? I mean—' Gillian spread her hands and looked around her '—you're pretty isolated here. You work here, live here—what other pleasure does he have?'

'None, I guess,' admitted Keisha.

'And he's not exactly the sort of man who'd live like a hermit. He's sex on two legs. He has a huge libido. I bet he's had his fill of girlfriends over the years. Is there anyone here?'

'Not that I know of,' answered Keisha.

'So you're his whole supply of love?'

Keisha laughed. 'Don't be so crude, Gillian.'

'Do you mind?'

'Mind what? Being his only lover?'

'Yes.'

'Of course I don't. I wouldn't let him touch me if I thought he was hopping from bed to bed.'

'So what's the situation?' Gillian looked at Keisha intently, a tiny frown furrowing her brow.

Keisha shrugged. 'I don't know. I don't think there's a chance we'll ever get back together, but—he turns me on. Is that a sin?'

'Not when the man's as gorgeous as Hunter,' declared Gillian with a wide smile.

'Is there a man in *your* life at the moment?' Keisha enquired, wanting to change the subject. Gillian flitted from one man to another with alarming frequency, never seeming able to find Mr Right.

'No, but you never know,' she confessed. 'I might find a charming Spaniard while we're over here. You've not met any eligible ones, have you, looking for an English redhead?'

Keisha had to confess that she hadn't. And after a light lunch they made their way down the winding track to the beach.

'Gosh, look at those fantastic boats!' exclaimed Gillian as they headed towards the marina. 'Millionaires' paradise! Which one is Hunter's?'

'He doesn't have one.'

'He doesn't?' Gillian's voice rose and her eyes widened. 'I'd have thought it was a better bet to have one here than in London. Hey, look at this. It's got your name on it.'

Keisha could hardly believe her eyes. *Keisha II*. There it

was. In all its glory. A beautiful streamlined ocean cruiser. Twice as big as his other one. 'I don't understand,' she said. 'Hunter's said nothing to me about having a boat here. It's probably just a coincidence, having my name on it.'

Gillian pooh-poohed the idea. 'It must be his,' she claimed excitedly. 'His boat on the Thames was named after you, wasn't it?'

Keisha nodded.

'There you are, then. He's clearly never got you out of his mind. Don't forget to invite me to the wedding.'

'Oh, Gillian!' exclaimed Keisha. 'It's never going to happen.'

But her friend merely grinned.

They strolled along the shore, catching up on all the gossip, and when they scrambled their way back up the mountainside they found that Hunter had returned.

Gillian, never one to keep her mouth shut, immediately said to him, 'Is that your boat—with Keisha's name on it?'

Keisha wished she hadn't said anything. If it was Hunter's, then he must have a very good reason for not telling her. She turned away, not wanting to see his expression, not even wanting to listen to his answer.

There was a second's silence before she heard him say quietly, 'Yes, it's mine.' And then he must have made some sort of gesture, because her friend didn't ask any further questions.

Gillian joined them for their evening meal, and afterwards Hunter summoned his driver to take her back to her hotel.

After she'd gone he said, 'She's quite something, your friend.'

Keisha nodded.

'You're so opposite to each other. You're quiet and—interesting, she's loud and brash.'

'We were schoolfriends. I've known her for ever. She's a good friend to me. We get on well.'

'I know,' he said quietly. 'And I'm glad you have someone to talk to. Was I on the agenda?'

Keisha was unsure how to answer. 'We did—talk about you a little—yes.'

His eyes twinkled. 'More than a little, I bet. Does she think you're a fool for coming out here?'

'Gillian thought I was a fool for leaving you,' answered Keisha with a wry twist to her lips.

His brows shot up. 'Really? And yet you didn't take heed?'

'Why should I? It was my life, not hers.'

'And what do you feel now?'

They were sitting outside, enjoying the last rays of the sun. Why, Keisha asked herself, did their important conversations always take place at sunset? 'I think,' she said slowly, reluctantly, 'that I'm enjoying your company more than I thought I would.'

'Is that all? Enjoying my company?' Brows rose in dramatic fashion. 'Which part of my company? Sitting talking, as we're doing now? Or when we make spectacular love?'

Keisha could feel colour reddening her cheeks, and prayed he wouldn't notice. As a schoolchild she'd been prone to blushing; it had been the bane of her life. But she'd grown out of it. There was only this man who could make her face glow now.

He smiled, slowly and confidently. 'Maybe I don't need an answer. Maybe it's there for me to see.' He took her hands and pulled her towards him, sitting her down on his lap, brushing her hair back from her face before kissing her flaming cheeks. 'You're such an innocent. It's what I love most about you.'

Love? He had used the word *love*. Was it a figure of speech? Or a declaration? Keisha remained silent, closing her eyes, very much aware of the throbbing heat of his body.

'So you spotted my secret?'

Keisha frowned.

'My new boat.'

'Oh, yes,' she admitted. 'It looks very lovely.'

'It is very lovely. Not an expression I'd use myself, but I know what you mean,' he added with an earth-shattering smile. A smile that did things to her that should never be allowed.

'Why didn't you tell me about it?' she asked.

'Because I was waiting.'

Again she drew her brows together. 'For what?'

'Until I thought you might trust me enough to let me take you out on it. There's not been a lot of trust between us, has there? And out there on the high seas there'd be no place for you to run.'

Keisha's lovely green eyes widened, but she said nothing. He was right about the trust thing. And she still didn't trust him.

'What do you think?' he said. 'Shall we go out on it tomorrow? Spend the whole day on board? Would you like that?'

'But your work?' she protested, using it as an excuse because panic had begun to set in. A whole day on the boat could possibly mean a whole day making love. And was that what she wanted?

Yes! screamed her body.

No! screamed her mind.

'It's not right.' Keisha's eyes shone a brilliant green. 'I can't let you pay me for something I'm not doing.'

'Then I'll deduct it from your salary,' he declared with a boyish grin.

Keisha couldn't help wondering why he had never been like this in the early months of their marriage. His work had been the most important thing in his life then. He'd rarely taken time off for pleasure—or so he would have had her believe. 'So what is your answer?' Hunter asked. 'Shall we spend the day at sea?'

Keisha nodded, and her smile was so heart-meltingly tempting that Hunter couldn't help kissing her. And of course the kiss led to other things. It led to him swinging her up into his arms and carrying her upstairs without breaking the contact.

It led to them making love the whole night through.

It led to him thinking that he might not have the stamina to take out his boat tomorrow, and that if he did they would perhaps need to spend their time in bed again.

One half of him exulted in what he saw as Keisha's capitulation, but part of him sensed that she was holding part of herself back. The physical side of their relationship—if it could be called a relationship—was getting better and better, but there was something deep down in her heart that she wasn't telling him. Of course he had no tangible reason for suspecting any of this; it was just something he felt.

He could be completely mistaken. It might be that she didn't want to get too close to him again. That she was asking herself what he wanted from her. It was a good job she didn't know, because she would be out of here faster than he could say her name.

Funnily enough he found himself not quite so sure that he wanted to destroy her. Without him realising it, she had begun to get beneath his skin again.

Not that marriage would work a second time around.

His lifestyle hadn't changed that much. He still worked hard; he found it difficult to delegate. He *liked* working; he liked his finger on every pulse. Which was all right for a single man, he acknowledged, but not, as he had discovered, for a married man. And it definitely wouldn't be right for a married man with children.

He had been thinking lately that he would like to marry again and start a family. But it would have to be someone very different from Keisha. She had hurt him badly when she'd run off with someone else. So badly he had been scarred for life. And, of course, it would have to be someone who could put up with his lifestyle.

What could be more perfect? thought Keisha, as she lay on the deck of Hunter's luxury cruiser, enjoying the sunshine. The Spanish mainland was just a blur in the distance; their only company was several circling seabirds and the occasional other boat.

She felt as if they were alone in the world. It was hard to imagine that a few short weeks ago she had been penniless and at her wits' end. This was luxury unimagined. And, whether or not it ended after her six months were up, she knew that it was something she would remember for the rest of her life.

Hunter was at the helm. He wore a pair of brief navy shorts and a white T-shirt that did little to hide his magnificent body. In dark glasses he looked powerful and mysterious, and even as she watched him through half closed eyes she felt a surge of need wash through her. It was ridiculous when they'd spent all night making love, but she couldn't get enough of him. It was almost as though she needed to make up for lost time.

'Keisha!'

She sat up and smiled. It was hard to believe how nice he was being to her, considering that she had run out on him, that she had hurt him, that she had disappeared out of his life as completely as it was possible to do so.

At the time she hadn't stopped to think how he might suffer. She'd been so obsessed with her own unhappiness that Hunter's feelings hadn't counted. As far as she'd been concerned he was the one who was in the wrong.

But look how good he'd been to her ever since that night of the party.

She didn't deserve it!

'Would you like to swim? I'll drop anchor.'

'Yes, please,' she said eagerly. Her body was cooked, though whether it was from the heat of the sun or from thinking about this man who was still capable of turning her life upside down, she wasn't sure.

They played in the water, Hunter teasing her with his body as he'd done once before, in his pool back in London, making her want him so desperately that her whole body ached. It was when he gave her a moment's respite, when Keisha was hanging on to the stern rail and looking at the sunlight sparkling on the water, that she thought she saw a dolphin watching them.

'You're fantasising,' declared Hunter when she told him.

'No, I'm not. I saw one over there.'

'But it wouldn't be *watching* us.'

'Yes, he was!'

'There are dolphins in these waters,' he admitted, 'and even sperm whales, but really, Keisha—'

And then together they both saw not one dolphin but a whole pod, and they watched in stunned delight as they leapt joyfully through the water.

And then they were gone!

Keisha clung to Hunter as they watched and waited in silence, but they didn't come back. It was a most moving experience, and the fact that they'd shared it made her feel even closer to Hunter. 'That was quite something,' she said with awe in her voice as they climbed back on board.

'And you're quite something too,' he growled. 'Come here. I want you.'

Their wet, cool bodies soon became hot and steamy. In the master suite, which was luxury like Keisha had never seen before, with a king-sized bed and a plasma television, and an *en-suite* bathroom even more luxurious than his one at home, Hunter took her out of this world and into the next. Into a world of senses and beautiful bodies and pleasures untold.

As he kissed her, and tortured her body with skilled fingers, Keisha felt sure that her bones were melting. Hunter was expert in drawing out her deepest emotions, in finding new places to touch and incite into exquisite excitement. Her limbs jerked and quivered, and the more he stroked and explored the more out of control she became.

'Take me, Hunter, please,' she begged, when she could stand his torment no longer.

He smiled mysteriously. 'All in good time, my darling! All in good time.'

Rarely had she known him to have such control over his body. He was most definitely a force to be reckoned with today. She rolled away from him, taking over the dominance, torturing him instead with hands and mouth, with tongue and teeth, he bucked and groaned, and in no time at all Hunter was the one who begged for relief.

Never had their final moments been so strong. Never had Keisha felt as though her body could stand no more intense pleasure. With Hunter deep inside her, completely at his mercy, she felt that she would explode from sheer unadulterated enjoyment.

It took a long time for their breathing to return to normal, and when it did Hunter asked quietly, 'What is happening to us, Keisha?'

CHAPTER TEN

KEISHA LOOKED AT Hunter with wide, luminous eyes, unaware that they had never looked more beautiful. 'There's nothing happening,' she said firmly, and although she would have liked nothing more than to remain in his arms she rolled away, turning her back on him and hunching her shoulders

She was in grave danger of becoming too deeply involved—and that could never happen. There was so much about her life that she had never told him—which would destroy them both. She simply couldn't afford to get emotionally involved.

His brows jerked together. 'You're regretting it already?'

'No! Yes! Yes, I *am* regretting it. I don't want to get involved with you again.'

'Liar!' He rolled off the bed and stood looking down at her.

Keisha almost felt like laughing. He was at his indignant best—but also totally naked. The two simply didn't go together.

'So it's purely sex you want from me, without obligation?' he asked, his voice rising. 'Is that all you've ever wanted?'

Keisha sat up and hugged a sheet over her breasts. 'Please, Hunter, don't spoil this moment. We've just made the most wonderful love ever. But I know we'll never commit again. Can't we—enjoy what we have?' The instant her words were out she regretted them. It made her sound as though all she wanted was his body.

Hunter instantly picked up on it. He spread his feet and folded his arms and stood over her like a jailer. 'What you're saying is that you're hungry for a physical relationship, but nothing more?'

'No!' she exclaimed. Put like that, it made her sound oversexed. As though any man would do. 'I'm not hungry for anything. But, Lord help me, I can't help myself when you're around.'

Hunter's lips slowly broke into a smile. 'Shall I let you into a secret? I can't help myself either. It looks like we have a problem.'

An insurmountable one, thought Keisha.

'But I think I know a way around it.'

'You do?' Keisha drew her brows together and looked at him curiously. Perhaps he was going to suggest they gave up the whole idea of living here and returned to England? She could then move into her own place, and they wouldn't need to see so much of each other.

He sat down on the edge of the bed and ran a gentle finger down the length of her nose, over her trembling lips, and Keisha knew then that her thoughts had been ridiculously wrong. He had something much more devious in mind.

'You do agree that we're getting on much better together?' he asked.

Keisha nodded.

'And not only physically?'

'Yes,' she said faintly, wondering what was coming next. Heaven help her if he was going to suggest that they get married again, because she couldn't do that. Not with all this anguish inside her. How she wished now that she had told him in the very beginning. The longer time went on the more difficult her confession was becoming.

A look of sheer amusement filled his face, lit up his eyes and widened his mouth. 'I think, Keisha, we should embark on an affair. I think we should behave as though we've only just met. Here, in this special place, I think we should learn to get to know each other all over again.'

He waited for her reaction, and when she did nothing but look at him in stunned silence he went on, 'I realise we both had our failings. It's something we need to work on. But I think we should at least give it a try. What do you say?'

Keisha didn't know what to say. His suggestion was like a bolt from the blue. Most certainly not expected, but tantalisingly tempting all the same. 'There's a lot we need to resolve,' she said faintly.

'I agree, but we have time. All the time in the world! We can take one tiny step at a time—if that is your wish.'

Still she had her doubts. He could be suggesting it so that she would feed his physical needs while they were working here. She had to put the question. 'How do I know you'll remain faithful to me? You had an affair while we were married. If temptation's put your way it will be much simpler now that we're free agents. And I couldn't put up with it.'

To her astonishment Hunter bounced to his feet again, and his eyes grew furiously dark. 'For your information I never touched another woman during our marriage, despite what you might think. And why, when I've just asked you to have an affair with me, would you think I might defect?'

'It's not impossible,' she suggested, with a wry twist to her lips. 'You attract the opposite sex like a flame does a moth. Even my friend Gillian said she wouldn't be averse to going to bed with you.'

Hunter shook his head. 'It looks like your opinion of me hasn't altered one iota. And since we're on the subject—' his voice grew more condemning '—how do I know that *you* won't take it into your head to run off again with another man?'

When she didn't answer, when she merely looked at him in bewilderment, he said in an even fiercer voice, 'Forget I asked you. I got carried away in the heat of the moment.' And he stamped off towards the bathroom.

Keisha felt as though she'd been slapped in the face, and immediately jumped off the bed and charged after him. 'What the hell are you talking about?'

'Don't think I didn't see you,' he snarled, his top lip curled and his whole body rejecting her.

'See me *what?*' she echoed, completely confused by now, and not finding it funny any longer that both of them were nude.

'With your arms around him—in broad daylight,' he snorted, cold criticism on his face. Anyone seeing them would have found it impossible to believe that only moments earlier they had thrown inhibitions to the wind and enjoyed the most wonderful sex.

Keisha was lost. 'I'm sorry; you must have mistaken me for someone else. I've never been with anyone since you.'

'Really?' His normally cobalt eyes were black with anger. 'Don't lie to me, Keisha, I saw you.'

'Where, for pity's sake?' she asked. 'When?' Her breast was heaving by now, her pulses stammering all over the place. There had to be some terrible mistake—but what? Hunter reckoned he'd seen her, but she'd never so much as talked to another man. Why would she when she'd still been getting over him? She'd wanted to steer clear of every male in the country.

'In Oxford Street, a couple of days after you walked out. Who was it? Marc Collins? Your so-called innocent male friend? Some friend he turned out to be!' His blazing eyes dared her to deny it.

'Ah!' Keisha let her breath out on a long enlightened sigh.

'So there was someone?' he jumped in quickly. 'I knew it. I knew you were lying. Get dressed, Keisha, we're going back.'

'Hunter!' Keisha put her hand out to touch him, but he jerked away and she felt so hurt that she wanted to cry. 'Listen to me. It was all perfectly innocent. It was—'

'Isn't that what they all say?' he demanded coldly.

'But it's the truth. It was my cousin,' she added lamely, all the fight suddenly going out of her. What was the point in defending herself when he was clearly not prepared to listen?

'Cousin?' But it stalled him, made him to turn to face her again, a frown as deep as the Grand Canyon furrowing his brow.

'Daniel and I grew up together. We were like brother and sister. Then he and my aunt and uncle emigrated to Australia. We were both shocked beyond belief when we bumped into each other. In Oxford Street of all places! With the thousands and thousands that pass through every day it was nothing short of a miracle.'

Hunter's eyes locked into hers as he seemed to be wondering whether to accept her story or not. He searched her face for long seconds. 'Is that the truth?'

She nodded and held her breath.

Gradually the tension went out of his body, and he held out his arms to her. 'I'm sorry, Keisha, for doubting you.'

'So all this time,' she said, as the full importance of what he'd said filtered through, 'you thought I'd left you for another man?'

He nodded.

She felt sad that he had thought so badly of her, and tears squeezed from her eyes. Instantly Hunter gathered her into his arms. 'Don't cry, Keisha. Don't make me feel a bigger fool than I am.'

'You should have come up to us, I would have introduced you,' she replied in a hurt little voice.

'I wanted to strangle you,' he confessed. 'Walking away was the hardest thing I ever did—and the most foolish. I realise that now.'

Keisha closed her eyes and shook her head slightly. It was difficult to take in. So much had happened that could have been solved if he'd spoken to her on that fateful day. Instead he'd walked away and lived the next three years believing she had been unfaithful to him. No wonder he hadn't made a more intensive search for her.

Three years of hating her, while she had spent three years still half in love with him, sometimes wondering whether she had made the biggest mistake of her life, whether her immaturity had been the main problem.

And now he had asked her to commit to him again. Well, almost. An affair. It sounded gloriously decadent.

She was older and wiser. Would it work the second time around, now that they had cleared the air? She loved him desperately, and there would never be anyone else for her, of that she was very sure. But would it really work?

'So, Keisha, where do we go from here?'

Keisha had never seen his eyes look so sad or so hurt, and her heart went out to him. 'I think, Hunter,' she said with a faint, anxious smile, 'that we should both get showered and dressed and then sit and talk. We can't have a serious conversation looking like this.'

'You're right,' he agreed. 'Though it does seem a pity to cover up your delectable body.' And he let his eyes slowly glide over her.

Keisha felt a renewed frisson of awareness. 'If I want to get any sense out of you then it's very necessary,' she replied. 'I'll go first.'

The shower cubicle was large enough to fit a family, with a massive gold shower head that massaged or pulsed or did whatever you wanted it to do, and Keisha wasn't altogether surprised when Hunter joined her.

It looked as though talking had gone out of the window. Hunter was talking with his hands, thrilling her, touching her in all the right places.

He played with the controls so that sometimes the water rained down heavily on them, while at others it was like gentle summer rain. And he suited his actions to the water pressure, turning the whole experience into something sensual and exciting.

She generally thought that his lovemaking could never get any better, but somehow he always found something different and electrifying to do. What a lot she would be missing out on if she rejected his suggestion of an affair.

On the other hand physical gratification wasn't everything. There was friendship and honesty—and, although they'd just overcome one hurdle, there were other things she needed to tell him.

At one time she had thought her miscarriage was the most important. It was still a big issue, and he would be far from happy, but the fact that she was infertile had suddenly loomed as much more significant. If their affair should turn into something more he would need to know. Long before anything serious developed. She couldn't hide such an essential issue from him.

Except that it would spoil things before they had even started. She could perhaps wait a little longer. Until she was surer he wasn't simply playing with her feelings.

Back on deck, an opened bottle of champagne sitting in front of them, a glass in her hand, and a pair of cotton shorts and a T-shirt covering her modesty, Keisha answered Hunter's question. 'Yes, Hunter, I will have an affair with you. In fact it sounds quite the most exciting proposition I've had in a long time.'

'Thank you, Keisha,' he said quietly. 'Have I told you how particularly lovely you're looking today? You're beginning to put weight back on, and you most certainly have a glow to your skin. You no longer look like a ghost.'

'Is that really what I looked like?' she asked with a wry smile.

'When I met you at the party, yes.'

'I guess I did feel a little wraith-like,' she admitted. 'And,' she added shyly, 'my transformation is entirely because of you.'

'Then I'm honoured. I think our affair will be a constant source of delight. I'd forgotten what a magical creature you are. I can't wait to take you to bed again.'

Already Keisha could feel her body tingling. What was it with this man? Somehow he managed to keep her in a constant state of readiness. She almost felt as though she'd died and gone to heaven. For the moment at least, until she unleashed her burden on him, life couldn't get any better.

Keisha's happiness shone in her eyes and they stayed out on *Keisha II* for the rest of the day, making small talk, touching, kissing, eating occasionally, making love frequently. They watched the sun go down in all its spectacular glory, and then, because neither of them could bring themselves to move, they spent the whole night at sea.

The king-sized bed, with its silk covers and sumptuous deep mattress, was a lovers' dream. It tempted them to sleep, but was also seductive enough to encourage them into further lovemaking.

Eventually they were both so exhausted that they fell into a long, deep sleep, not waking until almost noon the next day.

'I guess we should be heading back,' said Hunter reluctantly, after they'd eaten a breakfast of fresh fruit and yoghurt.

Keisha nodded.

'You've not changed your mind?'

'No,' she whispered, standing on tiptoe to touch a kiss to his lips.

Instantly he caught her to him. 'You've made me the happiest man alive—do you know that? Having an affair with you is going to be like opening Christmas presents when you're a child. A voyage of discovery! I'll never know what to expect next.'

They'd hardly been back an hour before Hunter was called to his Seville office. 'My darling, I'm sorry,' he said regretfully. 'There's a problem that needs my attention. I'll be as quick as I can.'

But Keisha was in an excellent mood. 'Don't rush on my behalf.' Her euphoria was such that she didn't care if he was away for the rest of the day. In fact she looked forward to spending time on her own. So much had happened that she needed space to think.

An affair sounded far more thrilling and sinful than simply agreeing to become lovers again. Cloak and dagger stuff! Whether anything would come out of it was not something she dared think about. She wasn't even sure whether she would want to marry Hunter again if he should ask her.

Only time would tell whether he would remain true. Time

that she needed, to face her own demons and work out how she was going to tell him. She couldn't even begin to imagine how angry he would be when she confessed that she had been carrying his child when she left. It could mean an end to everything. Ought she to face up to him now, before their relationship got too serious?

But when he didn't return home until well past midnight, and was off again at seven the next morning—a pattern he repeated for many days to come—Keisha was vaguely pleased that she hadn't told him.

He didn't deserve her honesty if he was going to fall back into his bad habits. She felt as if he didn't care any more now he'd got her to commit to him. Was it the chase he liked? Did he get bored once he had achieved his aim? Was he already on the lookout for another woman to charm?

'We have a big ad campaign coming up,' he said, by way of an explanation. 'The biggest by far—it means a lot to me. But—' he looked at her sorrowfully '—something has gone drastically wrong. They're threatening to pull out. I think we've been got at by competitors—and I don't intend losing that business if it's the last thing I do.'

'I see,' she said quietly. This campaign would clearly net him a small fortune—and making money was one of the most important things in his life.

For the moment more important than she was.

Maybe, she thought, as she sat by the pool one morning, his way of life would never change. It could be that this was a warning. That even indulging in an affair with him would be a mistake.

She was strongly tempted to leave. Only the fact that she was bound to Hunter because she owed him money kept her there. But she wasn't happy.

Admittedly he had a crisis on his hands, but she couldn't accept that he had to take total responsibility, that he needed to be at the office from eight until midnight—every day. He was like two different men. It was either all work or all play—there was no in between. And this was something she couldn't handle.

Or was she putting her own feelings, her own happiness, before his again? Was she the selfish one?

Keisha went up to the office and turned on the computer. She would find some work to do. There were several e-mails from Gillian, and one—to her surprise—from Hunter.

She opened it.

Just to remind you that I'm looking forward to our love affair!

That was all. She felt flattered that he'd found the time to send her this, and a whole host of emotions sprang up in her chest. It looked as though she'd badly misjudged him.

But when she looked at the date it was the day they'd returned from their boat trip. Since then—nothing. They'd not even made love. He was always too tired when he came in to do anything but go to bed and go to sleep. He held her in his arms, yes, but that was all.

By the time he came home that evening, however, her unkind thoughts had been pushed to the back of her mind. She had given herself a good talking to, stressing that she had to accept him for what he was. If he wanted or needed to work long hours then she had to put up with it. She had to accept that this was Hunter. This was his life. Surely she was old enough now, and woman enough, to make such allowances?

His eyes were shadowed, and he looked so tired and

drained that she ran him a bath in the big round bathtub and after a moment's hesitation got in with him. At first he was too exhausted to do anything other than lie back and relax in the scented water with his eyes closed. She'd poured in a drop of muscle relaxant, and it seemed to do the trick because after a while he pulled her closer to him and began nuzzling her cheek and stroking her breasts.

'I'm sorry that our plans have been put on hold,' he said softly. 'It wasn't my intention, you know that.'

'I know,' she said.

'Are you cross with me?'

'I hate being on my own,' she admitted. 'There's nothing to do.'

'Which means you *are* cross.'

'Can't someone else do the work?' she asked.

'I daren't trust anyone.'

Keisha closed her eyes. 'Daren't trust, or don't want to?' All her good intentions suddenly faded, and she let fly. 'You're the Mr Big I Am. Finger on every pulse! Afraid no one will do the job as well as you.'

'You really don't understand, do you?' he accused, nostrils flaring now, eyes as hard as polished sapphires. 'How important this campaign is to me? All you think about is yourself. Poor little Keisha, left alone all day. It doesn't matter that you're in a most enviable location, that most women your age would give their eye teeth to be in such a position. Grow up, Keisha, for goodness' sake.'

'Grow up?' she scorned, eyes glaring. He was really getting up her nose now. 'You've no idea what I've gone through because of you. None at all!' She stood up and stepped out of the bath, wrapping herself in a towel and heading for the door.

'What *you've* gone through?' He climbed out too, catching her by the shoulder and spinning her to face him. His voice was so harsh it was like sandpaper against her skin. 'Lady, I bailed you out of debt, I've given you a life of luxury—and you're daring to complain?'

'I almost lost my life because of you,' she cried in a spurt of anger.

Hunter went suddenly still. 'What the hell are you talking about?'

'I lost your baby and I very nearly lost my own life.' Immediately the words were out Keisha regretted them. This wasn't how she had meant to tell him. This was a disaster. For goodness' sake, why hadn't she kept her mouth shut? Not that she showed her fear. She stared at him defiantly instead.

There was silence in the room. A loud silence. They glared at each other like two raging bulls.

'When?' The word shot out like a bullet from a gun.

'Eleven weeks after I left you.' She felt the fight going out of her, felt her shoulders sagging, and she held on to her towel like a lifeline.

'And you're saying the baby was mine?'

She nodded.

'If that was the case why didn't you tell me?'

'I tried to, but—'

Keisha closed her eyes, despair filling her body. She had dreaded this scene. She'd known that some time she'd have to tell him, she'd even been rehearsing it, but to blurt it out like that was unpardonable.

They stood there for long moments, glowering at each other, until finally Hunter sagged on to the edge of the bed and put his face in his hands. 'Tell me it isn't true.'

'I can't,' she said, her throat thick and full.

She hated seeing Hunter like this. She wanted to go to him, to put her arms around him, tell him that she loved him—because she *did* love him, heaven help her!—tell him that what had happened in the past didn't matter, that if he would have her she would always be at his side.

Hunter felt as though he'd been beaten with a thousand sticks. Keisha had been carrying his baby and she'd never told him! *His* baby! His own child! His flesh and blood! How could she do this to him? How could she have kept something so life-changing a secret?

The fact that he'd been thinking before she'd walked out on him that he'd like to start a family made it all the harder to bear. He felt violated, and he hurt so much that he knew he would never get over it.

He didn't stop to think how she might be feeling, what she had gone through, he was too blazingly angry. He sprang up from the bed, his eyes burning with condemnation. 'How could you do this to me? How could you not tell me about my own child? What sort of a woman are you?'

'Our marriage was over,' she defended, her chin high, her eyes vividly emerald.

And even now, as angry as he was, he could not help but admire their beauty. They were one of Keisha's best features. He had often used to think about having a daughter with Keisha's eyes.

His nostrils flared. Maybe he'd had a daughter? Maybe the baby she'd lost had been a girl? 'What was it?' he asked thickly.

'I don't know. I was too ill to ask,' came her swift response. 'Maybe it was too soon to tell. I don't know.'

'And you don't damn well care, do you?' he rasped.

But then some of the fight went out of him. He was being unfair. Not that he could help it. When she dropped a bombshell like that what was he supposed to do? Cuddle her? Tell her how sorry he was?

That would come later. For the moment all he wanted to do was lick his own wounds. 'I think you'd best get out of here,' he growled.

Keisha needed no second bidding. She marched out of the room with her back straight and her chin still high. Proud and unrepentant, and still very beautiful!

CHAPTER ELEVEN

WHEN KEISHA GOT up the next morning Hunter was nowhere to be seen. His housekeeper, a grizzled elderly lady, who always dressed in black and scraped her iron-grey hair back in a bun—and who Keisha found extremely intimidating—told her in a mixture of broken English and mime that he'd left the villa in the early hours without even having any breakfast. And the look she gave Keisha seemed to suggest that she was the one to blame.

Keisha had always been aware that the woman thought the sun shone out of Hunter's eyes. Now she was confirming it, and she couldn't help wondering whether she had heard them arguing.

When he didn't come home that evening, or the one after, Keisha knew that any chance of them having an affair, or getting close in any way, was very slim to say the least. She had let him down big-time. He was telling her in the cruellest way possible that their relationship—if it could be called that—was over.

Perhaps it was just as well. Because even if they did make up, when she eventually plucked up the courage to tell him that she couldn't have any more children she would definitely be out on her ear.

She missed him so much, but the nights were the worst. She yearned for him in bed beside her. She'd never been with another man, never known another man's touch, and in her heart of hearts she knew that she wanted no one else. But the truth of the matter was that there was no chance of them getting back together.

There were two choices left open for her—she could either go home and try to forget all about Hunter, or she could go to his office and face him, get him to talk. To sort things out one way or the other. It would be the decent thing to do. Because of one thing she was certain: she couldn't go on like this.

The office won.

His receptionist recognised her and smiled. 'I'll ring through to Hunter and tell him you're here. Is he expecting you?'

Keisha shook her head. 'I thought I'd surprise him.'

'In that case go straight up,' she said. 'You know where his office is?'

Keisha nodded. But her steps slowed as she mounted the stairs. If she descended on him without warning what would his reaction be? Hunter wouldn't thank her for interrupting him when he was in the middle of a crisis. But then she firmed her chin. Why shouldn't she? They had much to discuss, and if he wouldn't come to her then—

She came to an abrupt halt when she saw Hunter through the partially open door to his office. He wasn't alone. His companion was very beautiful. Tall and slender, dressed in a mulberry-coloured designer suit, her glossy black hair cut stylishly short. She dripped jewellery, and Keisha could hear the faint purr of her voice as she almost draped herself over Hunter.

And he in turn was smiling into her face.

She felt sick! All her old suspicions came hurtling back with a vengeance. But then she told herself that she mustn't jump to conclusions. This could very well be a client. Someone Hunter needed to suck up to in order to get her business. And she would be doing him a disservice if she interrupted them.

She turned and left.

Nevertheless when she got back to the villa Keisha began to make plans for her departure. There was really no point in her staying any longer. Whether Hunter was involved with another woman or not he had made it abundantly clear that he was finished with her.

Using the computer, she checked on flights to London. To her disappointment there was nothing for a couple of days, and although she didn't want to stay here any longer Keisha knew she had no choice.

Sitting out on her balcony that evening, watching the sun set, she couldn't help thinking back to their honeymoon, when the world had seemed her oyster, when she had believed that she was the luckiest girl in the world.

Her lips twisted wryly—sunsets had always seemed to be associated with high spots in her life. Until tonight. Contrarily, it had never been more spectacular. She had never seen such vivid reds and golds, such deep purples, such a glorious mix of colours that intermingled and seemed to be putting on a display just for her benefit.

To cheer her up, perhaps?

Or to remind her of all that she was missing? All that could have been hers if things had turned out differently.

She really had been a fool, not contacting Hunter when she'd first discovered that she was pregnant. None of this would have happened then. They might even have made it up.

He would have come to her when she'd lost her baby; he would have supported her and loved her.

Now he was blaming her. And perhaps he was right. She'd been so stressed over their break-up that it could well have been what had caused her to miscarry. She had thought this in the days following her loss, when she had lain in her hospital bed and cried huge tears that had never seemed to want to stop.

And when she'd met Hunter again the sense of guilt had been one of the major factors in her not wanting to have anything to do with him. She had known that if they got back together she would have to tell him. But to do it so explosively had been sheer madness! It looked now as though she was about to lose him again!

She rang Gillian, feeling an overwhelming urge to talk to someone. But her friend was out. Never had she felt more alone in her life. And she felt sadder than ever as she climbed into bed that night.

Finally sleep overtook her, and she dreamt about Hunter. She dreamt that they were married and had two children—a boy and girl, twins—and they were playing with them in the garden. She was happier than she'd ever been; her life was complete. Hunter was swinging their son between his legs and throwing him gently into the pool. He was a fine little swimmer, and kept climbing out and asking for more. But on one occasion he didn't surface. He lay there face down in the water. She yelled out, and Hunter jumped in and scooped him up in his arms.

She woke up then, and discovered Hunter standing beside the bed, looking down at her. Her initial thought was that he had come out of his black hole and was prepared to talk. But as the shadows of sleep left her eyes she saw that he was just as angry as ever.

'Is running away your answer to everything?' he questioned, his voice hard and condemning, his eyes emotionless.

Keisha pushed herself up against the pillows. She was relieved that he had come home. She didn't care that he still looked angry with her, because now they could talk.

'I was young and immature,' she said, startled to feel her body surging into life. 'I didn't know what else to do. I felt so neglected that—'

'I'm not talking about the first time,' he growled. 'I'm talking about now.'

Hard navy eyes burned into hers, but Keisha didn't see anger, she saw need. She held her arms up to him in a last ditch attempt to win him back. 'Come to me, Hunter. Don't hate me any more.'

'Hate?' he echoed flatly. 'I don't feel hate. I'm disappointed in you. Frustrated. But I've never hated you, Keisha. You were the one who did the hating.'

He looked tired, she thought—as though he'd been up all night, as though he'd had no sleep for days. 'Hunter, let me hold you. I've missed you so much.'

His eyes closed, and she thought that she could see a glint of tears, but she couldn't be sure. Then they snapped open again, and they burned into her soul.

'You've missed me, and yet you've never tried to contact me,' he accused. 'You've never once phoned the office and asked how I was or what I was doing. You've never tried to say you're sorry. All you've done is make plans for your departure. That doesn't sound to me very much as though you still want me.'

Keisha's eyes widened. 'How did you find out I was leaving?

* * *

Lord, her eyes were so beautiful. Hunter had never seen them so huge or so incredibly luminous—or so deeply disturbed.

He'd seen them darkly angry; he'd seen them soft with love; he'd seen them filled with desire. He'd also witnessed them glowing in the aftermath of their lovemaking—they were so incredible then, big green orbs that very nearly filled her face.

But never like this. Hurt and shocked, almost fearful.

They tapped into the very heart of him, made him feel when he didn't want to feel.

Keisha had hurt him so deeply, deceived him so painfully, that he had thought he would never get over it. And he most certainly had never wanted to share a bed with her again. But seeing her like this, tiny and vulnerable, horrified that he had discovered her secret, he realised that he wanted to protect her.

Maybe not protect—because who did she need protecting from? Himself, of course. He hadn't treated her well, and still deep in his soul he wanted to crucify her for keeping from him something of such astounding importance. It was clearly this guilty secret of hers that had made her withdraw from him each time they were in danger of getting too close.

He couldn't believe she hadn't told him. But on the other hand he couldn't harden his heart against her defenceless little body. She was like a fawn parted from its mother, terrified to be alone in the big wide world.

Terrified of him!

That didn't make him feel good. He ignored her question, and with a groan sat down on the edge of the bed and pulled her against him. How he had missed her! Not until this second had he realised how much. He'd been in no fit state, though, to talk to her. But now he couldn't wait to feel her delectable sweet-scented body, to explore every inch of her, to incite in her some of the magic that made her so wonderfully his. He didn't need words. He was afraid to use them anyway. He didn't want anything to spoil this moment.

Afterwards—who knew what might happen? But for the moment the only thing uppermost in his mind was taking her.

He needed urgent release.

He'd been so uptight these last few days that he had thought never to feel like this again. He'd punished himself by working harder than ever. He'd even slept at the office, in a room that contained a bathroom and a bed for any such emergencies.

Keisha's lips parted willingly for his kiss, and against him he could feel her heart throbbing wildly. Neither of them spoke. Neither of them wanted to spoil whatever was about to happen.

She felt good in his arms. He had not realised until this moment how much he had missed her. Three years they'd been parted—three years in which he had bedded only two other women. Neither of them had he wanted to spend the rest of his life with. Keisha had ruined him for anyone else.

When she'd come back into his life—after his initial shock and his desire for revenge, after his discovery that he didn't really hate her as much as he'd thought he had—he had never wanted to let her go.

But he hadn't known about her secret then!

His arms tightened, and his mouth pressed even harder against hers, teeth grinding on teeth, until he forced himself to relax. But he hadn't finished. He pulled back and began stripping off his clothes with indecent haste, his eyes never leaving hers. All Keisha was wearing was a minuscule night-dress, and he tore that off with feverish hands.

She made not a murmur, watching him with her soulful

eyes, panting a little, perhaps a little puzzled, but wanting him as desperately as he wanted her. How could he ever let her go? She was so gorgeous, so beautiful, so tempting in every way.

He pushed to the back of his mind the guilt he felt at not being there for her when she lost their baby. It had been paramount in his thoughts during the last few days; it had tormented him beyond measure. He had wanted to return home and console her, but knew that it wasn't possible. Because in the middle of his torture was the anger he felt that she hadn't told him.

Even now, as the thought popped unbidden into his mind, he wanted, just for one split second, to break every bone in her body.

It was gone just as quickly.

He tasted her mouth instead. He drank in her eager sweetness, reacquainted himself with every soft inch of skin, with every curve and hollow. He felt her squirm at his touch, wriggle with excitement. She arched against him, touching him as well, feeling, stroking, inciting, until neither of them could contain their need any longer.

And when it happened, when Keisha climaxed simultaneously with him, it was like an explosion of fireworks. It was like a Catherine Wheel twirling round inside him. It was like a rocket shooting sky-high. He felt as though he would explode.

And he realised in that moment that he didn't want to let her go. Not now! Not ever!

No matter what she did or said to hurt him.

He needed her and wanted her.

It wasn't just that they were physically fantastic together. It was everything about her. She was his spiritual partner as well as his earthly one. They belonged together. They were soul mates. They had lost and found each other.

Here in this hot paradise he had made her his again—and that was how he wanted it to stay for the rest of their lives. He'd been foolish not to go after her on that fateful day in London. So very foolish. The guilt would live with him for ever.

Gradually they recovered their equilibrium. Their breathing slowed, their bodies relaxed and Hunter rolled over to look at her. She was incredibly lovely, with her face flushed and her eyes just as he had known they would be. So large, so radiant!

He touched a finger to her lips, feeling them tremble, watching sudden uncertainty take the place of contentment. And he knew what she was thinking.

'I'm not going to let you leave me, Keisha,' he said softly.

'How did you know I'd planned to go?' Keisha asked. A faint breeze blew in from the open balcony doors, billowing the muslin curtains, cooling her skin, making her shiver.

Hunter instantly pulled the white cotton sheet with its delicate lavender trimming over her naked body. 'Computers always leave traces. You should have thought of that.'

'You've been up there?' she asked, with a tiny frown creasing her brow.

Hunter nodded. 'Would you have told me?'

'No,' she replied, her lovely soft mouth pulling into an apologetic grimace.

Hunter kissed his first two fingers before touching them to her lips. 'Then it's a good job I found out.'

'Would you have come after me?'

'The mood I was in—the mood I've been in for days—no,' he confessed.

'Then it would have been the end for us?'

'I guess so,' he said, before crushing her against him. 'Life would have been empty without you, Keisha.' His voice was little more than a groan. 'I'd have gone out of my mind.'

'I'm glad you came,' she whispered.

'So, Keisha, what do we do now?'

He looked suddenly serious, and Keisha wasn't quite sure what he expected of her. She twisted her lips into a wry smile and took the plunge. 'I think I'd like—if you're agreeable— to carry on our affair.'

They'd hardly begun when disaster had struck. And although she was still consumed by guilt and fear over her infertility, it didn't seem right to tell him now. It really would be the end. If she could make Hunter fall in love with her again, *really* in love, then perhaps that love would be strong enough to stand the shock.

'I was being selfish. I realise that now,' she said softly and apologetically. 'I was thinking only of myself. I'm so sorry. I know how much you love your work. I won't complain again.'

He held her close and they remained locked in each other's arms, sometimes sleeping, sometimes doing nothing except listening to each other's breathing, until a new day broke.

When he didn't rush off to work straight away, when they sat and had a leisurely breakfast, Keisha asked, 'Has your work problem finally been resolved?'

'Almost. I think we're nearly back on track. I have an important meeting with my client a little later this morning. I should know the good news then.'

'I'll keep my fingers crossed,' declared Keisha. She was so happy she couldn't sit still.

'Would you like to come with me? After all, you are my P.A.'

Was she? Keisha had almost forgotten that. He hadn't

included her in any of this; she had no idea what it was about. She shook her head. 'I think it's something you should do alone.'

'So what are you going to do while I'm out? If this deal comes off then I shall take my client to dinner. I might be late back.'

'I understand,' she said.

'You won't mind?'

'No, because I shall know what you're doing. It was when you were away for hours on end and I didn't know whether you were working or privately entertaining some other woman that I got grumpy.' And she still had a vision of the beautiful lady in his office. But she didn't let it worry her. Hunter had just convinced her that she was the one he wanted.

He grinned and, getting up from his chair, pulled her to him. 'My little jealous darling! How could there possibly be anyone else? On the other hand, I do have women clients. Still not jealous?'

Keisha stood on tiptoe and kissed him. 'I'll keep the bed warm for you,' she promised. 'Whatever time you come home.'

Hunter's arms tightened. 'If this weren't so important I'd take you back to bed right now. I'll never be able to get enough of you, Keisha. You do know that?'

The throbbing intensity in his voice made her want to go to bed too. And when he eventually left she felt like dancing till she dropped.

Admittedly she'd been at this stage before, and her fairy-tale dream had crumbled. But this time she was going to make very sure that nothing happened to destroy their happiness. She wanted their affair to turn into something more.

She was deliriously in love with him again. All she had to do was convince him that he loved her too.

She swam a little; she went upstairs to the office and checked whether anything had come through from London needing Hunter's attention. And all in all the day passed very pleasantly.

Even though Hunter was late coming home she did not mind, because he more than made up for it. It never ceased to amaze her how ready she was for him—or he for her!

They went to sleep in each other's arms, but in the morning he shook her shoulder and woke her. 'I'm the world's most insensitive swine.'

'Whatever's the matter?' asked Keisha at once, sitting up and staring at him. 'What have you done?'

'You mentioned that you almost lost your life, and I was so angry that you hadn't told me about the baby that I totally ignored it. How could I? What must you be thinking of me?'

He looked so concerned, so horrified, that Keisha couldn't help but laugh. 'Don't worry about it.'

'But I am worried. I can't believe I blotted it out of my mind. Tell me what happened.'

'I went to hospital because I had bad stomach pains. I knew something was dreadfully wrong. The next thing I remember was the doctor telling me I'd almost lost my own life as well as my baby's.'

'You were alone? You had no one with you?'

'No one,' admitted Keisha huskily. 'The doctor asked me whether I wanted my husband, but I told him you were in London.'

Hunter cursed beneath his breath. 'And you thought I wouldn't come? Oh, Keisha, how could you? I'd have dropped everything.'

'I didn't know that, did I?' she asked quietly.

Hunter's fingers curled into fists, and she could see the battle he was having with himself. She put her hands over his. 'Don't beat yourself up about it. It's done with now.'

'So what exactly went wrong?'

'I don't know, except that I'd never felt such pain in my life. I understand I have the doctors to thank for saving me.'

'And I thank them too,' he declared fervently. 'In fact I'd like to go there and do it in person. I blame myself entirely.'

'There is one other thing,' began Keisha, knowing that this was the perfect time to explain what else the doctor had said to her. Her heart hammered hard within her breast but before she could even begin, the phone interrupted her.

After Hunter had finished his conversation, he said ruefully, 'I have to dash. I'm needed. I'm sorry.'

'Why can't your people over here deal with things themselves?' she asked.

'They would do, if I weren't here,' he admitted. 'They'd have to. I think they're a little afraid of me, to tell you the truth. Afraid I might find they're not doing their job properly. I'm not an ogre, am I?'

The look on his face made Keisha laugh. 'I see nothing more than a hugely sexy man—someone who drives me mad with lust. Do you have time before you go?'

'I wish,' he said, with such longing that Keisha laughed again.

After breakfast she trekked down the hill to the shore and wandered over to Hunter's magnificent vessel. *Keisha II*. She smiled as she read its name, and she put out her hand and stroked the painted surface. It was as smooth as silk, sensuous to the touch. Even feeling it made her think of Hunter and what he could do to her. And what magnificent love they had made on board.

She felt tempted to climb up and sit on the deck, and let

her thoughts wash over her, but then felt it would be silly and far too sentimental.

'So here you are.'

Keisha turned and saw Hunter, and felt a quick surge of happiness.

'I've been looking for you. I want to share my good news,' he said. 'I've regained the order, and we're going to celebrate. I'm going to throw a big party at the villa and you, my darling, will be my stunning hostess. I'm going to show you off to everyone.'

He paused for a moment, looking deep into her eyes, and then added, 'I was wondering whether you'd agree to wear this?'

CHAPTER TWELVE

As SOON AS Keisha felt Hunter slipping a ring on her finger she squealed and snapped her eyes open. It was the biggest diamond ring she'd ever seen—and it fitted her perfectly.

'It's gorgeous Hunter, but—'

'No buts,' he declared firmly.

There was a but: a big one. How could she agree to marry him when she had such a huge confession to make? It hung over her head like an executioner's axe. She wished now that she had come out into the open long ago. Except that if she had he wouldn't be asking her to marry him for the second time. She would never experience this delirious happiness.

Nevertheless she must tell him. *And she must do it now!*

'Hunter, I—'

'Are you saying that you don't want to marry me?' he asked fiercely, taking her by the shoulders and looking deeply into her eyes.

'Of course not. It's just I have—'

'Then whatever it is it can wait,' he declared peremptorily. 'Today is special; I want nothing marring it.'

And when he kissed her Keisha let her fears fade into the background. For how long she didn't know, but at least he was giving her a temporary reprieve. She would wait until after the party. He was so rapturous about winning his advertising campaign back that it would be cruel of her to spoil it.

Hunter wanted to call in a party planner, but Keisha would not hear of it. 'You can get caterers to do the food,' she said, 'but that's all. I want to do everything else myself. It will give me something to do while you're at work.'

'I'm not going to the office,' he reminded her. 'The emergency is over. I'll be working here from now on. And you, my beautiful darling, will be working with me.'

Nevertheless Keisha insisted on doing the organising. It made her feel useful and needed. She had sat around for too long. She strung pretty lanterns through the trees and tied ribbons everywhere. She organised a three-piece band and arranged for a deck to be erected for dancing.

She spent a whole morning on the phone hiring tables for the food, fridges for the drinks, glasses, plates—everything she could think of. The terrace was transformed, and she even got the gardener to help clear one of the rooms inside, just in case it rained.

'This isn't England,' Hunter reminded her with an indulgent smile. 'We can rely on the weather here. The forecast is perfect.'

And then he took her shopping for a dress, when she ruefully declared that she hadn't got anything nice enough to wear.

'I should have thought of that before,' he said instantly when she told him. 'I'll buy you a whole new wardrobe.'

But Keisha didn't want a new wardrobe; she wanted just one dress!

In the designer boutique that Hunter ushered her into she was shown dress after dress, trying each one on for Hunter's approval. Sometimes a look of horror would cross his face, and sometimes he'd turn his mouth down at the corners and ponder. He made her laugh, and he went through a whole range of expressions before one particular dress brought a huge smile to his face.

'Perfect,' he declared. 'You look like a dream, my darling. You'll knock them all dead.'

It was the essential little black dress—with a difference. There was nothing demure about it. It dipped in a vee at both the back and the front, and the narrow straps were made entirely of black pearls. The calf-length hemline was cut like the petals of a flower, with even more pearls decorating it.

It cost a fortune, and Keisha was horrified, but Hunter insisted. It was not the only thing he bought her either. More dresses were lined up, and by the time he had finished she'd ended up with the new wardrobe she didn't want.

'You spoil me,' she said, pouting up into his face.

'You're worth it,' he declared. 'I want to give you the world. I want to make up for everything that's gone wrong in our relationship.'

'Money won't do it,' she declared, a shadow darkening her eyes. 'I just want you, Hunter. Nothing else. Money doesn't mean a thing to me.'

He groaned and pulled her to him, right there in the middle of the shop. 'You're an incredible woman, do you know that? I must have been a fool to let you go.'

And she was even more of a fool, because she thought everything was going to be all right.

The day of the party Keisha was kept busy, making sure that all was going to plan. She'd perfected everything down to the last detail, not wanting to fail Hunter. And even though it was

the first time she'd done anything like this she was very happy
with the results.

Hunter was pleased too, and when she'd finished getting
ready, when the dress was in place and her hair fixed in several
plaited loops, finishing in a neat coronet on the crown of her
head, he surprised her by handing her a black leather box
edged in gilt.

'Open it,' he urged, when she stood staring down at it.

Keisha's heart missed a few beats when she saw the pearl
necklace and earrings that perfectly matched the dress. 'Oh,
Hunter, they're beautiful,' she said huskily. 'I had no idea. Put
them on for me, please.'

She stood with her back to him, watching him through the
mirror as he carefully fastened the necklace. His hands slid
possessively beneath the top of her dress, discovering breasts
that were free of any restraint.

'Hunter!' she squeaked. 'Please don't!'

'You don't want me to touch you now?' he asked with
mock indignation, tweaking her nipples between thumb and
forefinger, shooting huge frissons of desire through every
inch of her.

'Oh, God, I do,' she cried huskily, dropping her head back
against him and giving herself up to the sensations he evoked.
'But we have a party to attend. The guests will start arriving
in a minute.'

'To hell with the guests,' he groaned, sliding the dress off
her shoulders and taking her nipples into his mouth instead.

Such sweet, sweet pleasure! Such torment! Keisha felt she
was going crazy. 'You must stop—please, I can hear voices.'

With reluctance he did so. When she darted a glance at
their reflections Hunter looked like a very satisfied man—and
she was positively radiant too.

'Perfect,' he declared. 'You'll be the most dazzling woman there. And don't forget that was a taste of things to come. I might even give you a few more tasters during the course of the evening.'

'Hunter!' Keisha was scandalised. 'You can't do that! Not with people around us.'

'Watch me,' he warned, with yet another of his beautiful smiles.

He was such a gorgeous, gorgeous man, thought Keisha, wondering not for the first time why no other woman had snapped him up during their years of separation.

The party began well enough. Hunter introduced her to various members of his staff, to clients and to business colleagues. So many people, so many names. But they were all eager to meet her, telling her what a fine man Hunter was, and how pleased they were that he was going to get married.

No one knew that they'd been married before. No one cared. They were simply delighted to see two people so much in love. And, true to his promise, whenever he got the opportunity Hunter would touch her intimately, reigniting her flames, making sure that she looked every inch a woman in love.

'You're beautiful,' he whispered constantly in her ear.

Or sometimes he would say, 'You're incredibly sexy, do you know that?'

Whatever he said, however he touched her, she'd fill with the most beautiful feelings—amazing feelings, feelings that made her want to drag him up to their bedroom and make love.

When Keisha saw Hunter looking repeatedly towards the gate, when she saw him glancing at his watch, she touched his arm. 'Are you expecting someone else?'

He smiled and nodded. 'My most important guest of the evening! Dolores Moreno. The lady whose business was almost snatched from me!'

'I see,' said Keisha, and found herself also watching for this woman who had inadvertently caused so much dissension between them.

When she finally arrived Keisha sucked in her breath. She was a lady of outstanding beauty. Almost as tall as Hunter, regally elegant, wearing an emerald designer dress that clung slavishly to her voluptuous figure.

And she had seen her before!

'Keisha, I want you to meet Dolores Moreno,' introduced Hunter proudly. 'My biggest and most valuable client.'

And to Dolores he said, 'This is Keisha, my fiancée. The most beautiful girl in the world.'

'Your fiancée?' Dolores's perfectly smooth brow developed a faint frown, and when she took Keisha's hand it was but a perfunctory touch. 'I wasn't aware that you even had a girlfriend.'

She looked distinctly put out, and Keisha knew why. *This* was the woman she had seen drooling over him in his office.

This woman had designs on Hunter!

Even as this thought hit her Keisha's mind flew back to the late nights he had been keeping, and she wondered, just briefly, whether any of his time had been spent with this very beautiful lady. It probably had, she thought, and jealousy seared through her like a red-hot knife.

Dolores was Spanish through and through, extremely good-looking, with beautiful dark brown eyes that at this moment were speaking volumes. She clearly didn't like to think that Hunter was spoken for!

'Come,' she said to Hunter now, tugging at his arm. 'Come and get me a drink.' And he was whisked away from her.

The woman's perfume lingered, though. And she'd smelled it somewhere before.

When she looked for Hunter, wanting to ask the woman what it was called, he and Dolores had disappeared. And the next moment she was whirled on to the dance floor by one of their guests.

Male after male claimed her for a dance, and by the time the buffet was served Keisha was exhausted. She still hadn't seen Hunter or Dolores again.

She found a chair and sat down with a glass of wine—and then she remembered where she had smelled that perfume.

The whole scene came back to her with remarkable clarity. It had been in the early days of their marriage—before they'd split up. He'd come home late one night and she'd smelled perfume on him.

This perfume!

Admittedly it could be coincidence. It was probably sold worldwide. Millions of women could be wearing it. But for some reason Keisha didn't think it was coincidental. Dolores had been in England. Hunter had been seeing her even then!

And when he rejoined her, when that same perfume clung to his collar, jealousy as swift and dangerous as a poisoned arrow stabbed into her heart.

She couldn't even speak. This couldn't be happening. Not when everything was on the verge of falling back into place. Not when she'd had dreams of an entire lifetime spent together with the man she loved. She had to be mistaken.

But just then she caught sight of Dolores, and she looked like the cat who'd got the cream. She wandered out of the villa with her lipstick fresh and not a hair out of place. She'd clearly done a quick repair job, thought Keisha waspishly.

'Keisha, what's wrong? You look very pale all of a sudden.' Hunter tilted her chin and looked with concern into her face.

'It's nothing. I have a headache,' she lied.

'It's overwork,' he declared. 'You should have let me get someone in. I knew it was too much for you.'

'I think I'll take a couple of pills and go and lie down for a while,' she said, trying to avoid his eyes. It was a sheer impossibility. He looked so concerned that she could almost believe that she'd been mistaken.

Nevertheless she needed space; she needed time to herself. She needed to assess whether she was seeing something that wasn't there, or whether Hunter truly was secretly seeing this other woman.

He took her up to her room, made sure she was comfortable, and promised to return within the hour to see how she was. As soon as he'd gone Keisha jumped off the bed and found a window overlooking the party.

Her eyes scanned the throng of happy partygoers until she found Hunter—and as she'd suspected Dolores was at his side. She wasn't exactly clinging to him, and there was space between them, but she constantly looked into his eyes and her body language told Keisha that she wanted much more.

Feeling sick now, Keisha lay down again—and when Hunter came to see her she pretended to be asleep. He could tell their guests whatever he liked. She wasn't going down there again tonight. If she did she would scratch the other woman's eyes out.

At this point in her thoughts she realised that she was playing right into Dolores's hands. What she ought to do was go down there and claim him!

As this thought hit her mind she sprang off the bed. She splashed her face with cold water, rearranged her hair and renewed her lipstick, then with her chin high she went back to the party.

When she walked up to Hunter and Dolores she slipped her hand into his and smiled up into his face. She saw his swift jerk of surprise, followed by a delighted smile. 'You're feeling better?'

He looked genuinely pleased that she'd rejoined them, and Keisha smiled brilliantly as well. 'Much better, thank you.'

Out of the corner of her eye she saw the displeasure on Dolores's face, the way her nostrils flared and her lips clamped briefly together. It was gone in an instant, replaced by a weak smile. 'Hunter told me you weren't feeling too well. I'm glad you made it back.'

Glad indeed! Her comment was as false as her smile. Keisha ignored her, clinging on to Hunter instead. 'We haven't had a dance yet, darling.'

With a swift apology to Dolores he whisked her on to the floor, and after that she wouldn't let him go. Right through the evening they danced, resting occasionally, quenching their thirst with nothing more exciting than lemonade—Keisha wanted to keep a clear head for later!

And when the flamenco dancer she had hired came to give her performance Keisha insisted on sitting beside Hunter, trying to ignore the fact that Dolores had chosen to sit on the other side of him.

She was glad when the evening finished. All this false gaiety was taking its toll. And when the final guest had left, when Dolores had taken her lingering leave of Hunter, whispering something in his ear that brought a smile to his lips, she felt like a rag doll.

She dropped limply on to a seat. 'I'm exhausted,' she declared.

'And is it any wonder, my darling? You've kept up wonderfully considering your headache. Has it truly gone?'

Keisha put a hand to her brow. 'No!' It actually felt worse now than it had before.

'Then you go on up to bed and I'll be with you shortly.'

'Can't you come now?' she pleaded, fearing that even now he might go after Dolores.

'I thought you'd prefer to lie quietly.'

'I want you,' she said, putting as much passion into her voice as she could. Even though she knew that it wasn't his body she wanted tonight—it was an explanation.

As soon as they reached the bedroom Keisha turned to face him. Somehow she managed to keep her voice low and steady, knowing that to yell at him would get her nowhere. 'Is there something you're not telling me?'

Hunter frowned. 'I don't think so. What are you talking about?'

'You and Dolores?' she suggested.

'Dolores? You think there's something going on between us? Goodness, she's nothing more than my very best customer.'

'But she wants more? Is that it?' persisted Keisha.

'You're imagining things, darling. I can assure you that—'

'You can assure me of nothing,' she butted in relentlessly, throwing caution to the winds now. 'She's the same woman you were seeing in London, isn't she? The person who you claimed to be *entertaining* one night, saying she was a client! And that night I smelled her perfume on you! Well, maybe she *is* a client, but she's certainly something more to you as well. Even a fool can see that.'

When she had finished she collapsed on the bed, with her

eyes filled with tears and a black hole where her heart should have been.

Hunter looked at her sadly. 'Do you really think so badly of me, Keisha? Do you not trust me one little bit?'

'Can you deny that Dolores is in love with you? Can you deny that she's the one you've been spending so much time with recently?'

When she saw the defensive look in Hunter's eyes she knew that she was right, and she turned away from him, her shoulders bent, all the fight suddenly going out of her.

'Keisha! My sweetheart! Don't do this to yourself.' He rolled her over to face him. 'It's true Dolores fancies herself in love with me,' he admitted reluctantly. 'She has for years. But it's most definitely not reciprocated. I'm nice to her, yes—I want her business—but as for anything else, forget it.'

Keisha turned to face Hunter and saw nothing but open honesty in his eyes. She wanted to believe him, she really did, but she knew that if she were wrong her heart would be broken for ever. 'But that time in London when I smelled her perfume on you?' she persisted. 'How do you explain that?' Hearing the words leave her mouth, Keisha realised how pathetic they sounded, and buried her head in her hands.

'Your imagination will be the death of you, Keisha,' Hunter warned sternly. 'I was preparing an advertising campaign for her new perfume. She sprayed me with the damn stuff—said I needed to know what it was like before I could promote it.'

Keisha closed her eyes. Had she really got it all so badly wrong? Hunter had never lied to her before, and deep down in her heart she knew that he was telling the truth now. 'I can assure you,' he said, 'that I have never taken Dolores to bed. Why would I want to do that when I have you? You light up my life, Keisha. You make my body alive. Without you I am nothing.'

Keisha smiled and gently placed her hand on Hunter's cheek. She loved this man so completely, and knew she had wasted too many years believing him to be unfaithful, when he was the most solid person in her life. 'I believe you, Hunter, and I'm sorry for doubting you. Just seeing you together and smelling her perfume brought back so many painful memories. But let's forget it now and put the past behind us.'

'I agree,' Hunter said softly. 'But you still don't seem totally convinced by my fidelity,' he continued, a faint smile curving his firm mouth. 'Perhaps I should show you exactly how much you mean to me?'

And he did. He even found new and inventive ways to excite and thrill. Finally Keisha was content.

The following morning when she woke Hunter was already up, and when she went outside Keisha discovered that everything was back to normal. There was no trace of the party.

Hunter crept up behind her and wrapped his arms around her waist, nuzzling her neck. 'Good morning, Keisha!'

'Who did all this?' she asked. 'I was going to help.'

'You've already done enough. Did you sleep well? No more fears?'

'None at all,' she said with a smile, remembering how he had brushed those fears away last night.

'I have to go out for a while,' he confessed, still nibbling her neck. 'But I won't be long. You will be OK? It's purely business, I promise.'

'Hurry back to me,' she whispered.

Hunter had totally convinced her that she was his one true love, and she wasn't afraid any more that she might lose him. At least not on account of another woman.

But he hadn't been gone very long when she had a visitor.

'Dolores!' acknowledged Keisha, when the woman was shown into the room where she sat reading the morning paper. Her heart lurched inside her breast. Now what? She stared coolly at the woman standing in front of her.

Dolores wore a black suit with a silk lavender camisole, and looked the epitome of elegance. In contrast Keisha was in a pair of brief cotton shorts and a T-shirt. 'This is a surprise,' she said, endeavouring to keep the hostility from her voice. 'Hunter's not in, if it's him you came to see.'

'Actually, it's you I want to talk to,' answered Dolores. Her heavily made-up brown eyes were less than friendly. They were cool and assessing, and Keisha was instantly on her guard.

She allowed her brows to rise faintly, suggesting she couldn't imagine what her reason might be. 'Then do sit down. Would you like a drink? Some coffee, perhaps? I can—'

The woman cut her off abruptly. 'No, thank you. I shan't be staying long. I just want to tell you that I shall never give up on Hunter. And perhaps you don't know it, but he's far too sophisticated for the likes of you,' she added, with a curl of her top lip.

'Really?' asked Keisha, feeling anger rising swift and sharp. 'Then you won't have a very long wait, will you?' She flashed the diamond on her finger. 'We're getting married just as soon as it can be arranged. Maybe you'd like to come to the wedding? In fact I'm sure Hunter will invite you, considering how close you two have become lately.' She paused a moment for effect, and then added, 'On a purely business basis, of course.'

'Is that what he told you?' asked Dolores, lifting her finely shaped brows. 'But of course he'd want to protect you, wouldn't he? You're very naïve, though, if you think Hunter and I could spend so much time together and not do anything about it. He's such a highly sexed man.'

Keisha was so positive of Hunter's love for her now that she felt like laughing. 'You've known Hunter for a long time, haven't you? You met him in London, I believe? Three or four years ago?'

'That's right,' agreed Dolores. 'When I understand you were married to him for the first time?'

So he had told her. Up until this point Keisha hadn't been sure. 'So why didn't you get your claws into him after we divorced?' she asked coolly. 'No—don't answer. It's because Hunter has never returned your so-called love, has he? He's always loved *me*. We made a mistake when we parted. But do you know what, Dolores? It was worth it. Love the second time around is so much better. No one will ever separate us again. We're deeply and irrevocably in love.'

Dolores stared at her for several long seconds, the wind taken out of her sails, and then she spun on her ridiculous high heels and left the room.

Keisha wanted to jump up and sing. But she had to restrain herself until Dolores was out of earshot. Once she'd heard her car go, though, she danced around the room, her face alight with pleasure. And when Hunter came home she was still on a high.

He didn't ask why she was so happy, and she didn't tell him about her visitor, knowing that he naturally assumed it was because she was now confident in his love.

Which she was.

And always would be.

Except that she still had a confession to make. Something she had to do sooner rather than later. Something that might change his mind about marrying her.

CHAPTER THIRTEEN

'HOW MANY CHILDREN do you want, Keisha?' Hunter enquired softly.

Tonight had been one of those occasions when he had taken his time making love to her. Firstly he had kissed every inch of her body, following his exploration with devastating hands and knowledgeable fingers, until finally, when her body had felt that it could take no more, he had mastered her. Quite beautifully!

Now they both lay hot and exhausted on the bed, his arm across her, his breathing lifting her hair, fanning it, making it feel almost like another caress.

'I was thinking of perhaps three myself,' he went on. 'With at least one boy to carry on the family business! I think we ought to start making babies as soon as we're married, don't you?'

Keisha felt a hard knot develop in her stomach, and for a moment she could say nothing.

Hunter rolled on his side and looked at her, stroking a gentle finger down her nose. 'Doesn't the idea appeal? Do you want to wait awhile? I—'

'There's something I have to tell you.' Her voice came out as a scratchy whisper, and she had never been more afraid in her life. This was a make-or-break moment.

Hunter frowned faintly. 'Fire away. But don't tell me you don't want kids. Because—'

'Hunter, it's not that.'

She saw his relief and felt even guiltier.

'It's that—that I can't have children.' There—she had said it! All her months of agonising were over. But she didn't want to see his face, his hurt, his disappointment, so she turned away, hunching her shoulders and screwing her face up tight to stop the tears.

She felt him stiffen, sensed his anger, and she cursed herself for letting things get this far.

'How long have you known?' came the quiet question, his voice carefully controlled.

'Since I—lost my baby,' she confessed, curling her fingers, desperately wishing herself a million miles away.

'So why didn't you tell me?' Still there was no emotion in his voice.

'I did try a couple of times,' she admitted. 'But you were in no mood to listen. I can't marry you without telling you, though, and I'm very sorry if I've let you down. If you want to forget the whole thing I'll understand.'

There was a long silence. So long that she knew their relationship was doomed. Tears rolled down her cheeks and she curled herself into a tight ball. She wanted to die.

But finally he spoke. 'Keisha, don't beat yourself up.' He touched her shoulder and forced her to look at him. But his face had gone white beneath his tan, and she knew that he was deeply hurt. 'It's my fault as much as yours.'

Keisha frowned, unable to understand his logic. This was something she hadn't anticipated. She had expected harsh words and recrimination. She had thought he would jump off the bed and tell her to get out of his sight, that he never wanted to see her again. 'H-how can it be your fault?' she asked faintly.

'Because I was the one who made you pregnant! And you probably miscarried because of the stress of us parting. If I hadn't worked so hard, if I hadn't made your life such hell—'

'Hunter, it was not your fault,' she protested. 'And I'm so desperately sorry. I meant what I said about us not getting married. I can't give you what you want. It wouldn't be fair. And I'm sorry again that I didn't tell you earlier.' Tears rolled down her cheeks and she sobbed uncontrollably.

Hunter pulled her into his arms and waited until she had regained her composure. 'Keisha, I love you—not what you can do for me. I don't want to live without you. I want to marry you. I want you by my side for the rest of my life. Maybe the doctors got it wrong. We'll go and see the best gynaecologist money can buy. Whatever's to be will be. But at least I'll still have you.'

Keisha started crying again. She had never in her wildest dreams expected him to be so understanding. 'I love you, Hunter,' she sobbed.

'And I love you, my darling, and I want no more talk of you letting me down. None of it was your fault. All I wish is that I had been there for you. I'm still angry that you never sent for me. Especially after what you've just said. It must be the most devastating thing a woman can ever be told.'

Keisha swallowed the house-sized lump in her throat and nodded.

'And you went through it all by yourself. My brave sweetheart.'

He held her then, and they went to sleep like that, and when she woke the next morning he was still holding her.

* * *

And so their wedding was arranged, and the day dawned bright and clear. Keisha had never been happier. Gillian was going to be her bridesmaid, and had arrived two days earlier, and they'd gone shopping for her dress.

Keisha had already bought her own outfit, but she was keeping it a secret from Hunter. She wasn't wearing white this time, but something simple and elegant—and of course fabulously expensive. Hunter had given her a credit card and told her to spare no expense.

They were getting married in the garden. A white wooden gazebo had been erected, decorated with ribbons and flowers, and padded seats were set out in front of it. With its far-reaching views over the ocean Keisha could never have dreamt of a more romantic setting.

She found it hard to believe that Hunter had taken her devastating news as well as he had. She really had thought that it would be the end of her hopes and dreams. It proved how very much he loved her—more than she had ever dared hope.

When the wedding guests began to arrive Keisha couldn't help wondering whether Dolores would be amongst them. But she didn't really care. She was happier than she'd ever been.

And when they exchanged their vows, when Hunter looked into her eyes and she saw his utter devotion, she felt that she would faint from sheer joy. He was such a good man; how could she have ever doubted him?

She knew in her mind that he would never stop working long hours and settle down in the conventional way, but it didn't scare her any longer. He loved her unconditionally—that was all that mattered. And she loved him in exactly the same way.

'Well, Mrs Donahue the second,' said Hunter, after their guests had finally gone. 'How does it feel?'

'I love you,' she said fervently, her eyes so brilliant that they dazzled. 'I'll never run away again. I feel privileged, actually, that you still wanted to marry me after—'

'Shh!' He put a finger to her lips. 'Let's not talk about it today. Let's go and do what I've been wanting to do ever since I saw you in that gorgeous outfit.'

It was an ivory two-piece, made of silk and covered with fine lace. Keisha had put on a few pounds recently and she looked stunning in it. She wore a tiny circle of lace in her hair and ivory high heels.

'You are so beautiful, my darling. I can't wait to get my hands on you.'

And make babies, she thought. It was what he'd planned! She felt sad for a moment, but then realised how lucky she was that he'd accepted the fact.

They were going to spend their honeymoon in Madeira, in the same hotel they'd gone to the first time, and then fly back to London, where Hunter wanted her to see a gynaecologist.

'Well, Mrs Donahue, I'm not altogether sure why you're here.'

Keisha looked at Hunter anxiously, clinging on to his hand, knowing that the specialist was going to say there was nothing he could do. She could feel tears threatening already, and she wished now that she had never gone through with the marriage. It wasn't fair on Hunter.

'I'm sorry,' she whispered to him.

He squeezed her hand tightly, trying to reassure her, but she could see the lines of tension round her mouth.

'I have all the notes from when you lost your baby, and I know what they told you. But the truth of the matter is...'

He paused for a moment, and Keisha wanted to scream at him to get on with it.

'They got it wrong.'

Oh, goodness—was this going to be even worse than she had thought?

'There's no question of you not being able to have children, Mrs Donahue. In fact, it's my pleasure to tell you that you're pregnant,' he announced with a broad smile. 'May I be the first to congratulate you?'

Keisha's mouth fell open. 'I can't be!'

'I can assure you,' said the gynaecologist, 'that you are— very much so. And both you and the baby are very fit and healthy.' He held out his hand.

She shook it faintly, still in a daze, and then she turned to Hunter, who looked equally stunned. They both broke into wide smiles and hugged each other, and got up danced around the room. The gynaecologist probably thought they were mad, but they couldn't help it. They were so relieved and happy.

'It's a miracle,' she declared.

'Miracles do happen,' confirmed the doctor. 'I've seen it before. Not often, but believe me they do happen. I'm very pleased for you both. I'll leave you to congratulate each other. There's no rush to leave.'

When they had the room to themselves Keisha looked into Hunter's beautiful cobalt eyes and shook her head in wonder. 'It truly is a miracle.'

'You're a clever lady, Mrs Donahue.'

'I can't believe it—not after what they told me. You must be very special, Hunter, to do this to me.'

'You are the special one, my sweetheart. You've just made me one hell of a happy man. Not that I wasn't before, you understand. But this is the icing on the cake. The pinnacle of my happiness! I love you, Keisha—more than life itself. I'm honoured that you believed in me enough to marry me a second time. And I'm proud that you're going to be the mother of my child.'

His arms tightened around her, 'Oh, Keisha. Let's go out and tell the world!'

Seven months later Keisha and Hunter were the proud parents of twins—a boy and girl, James and Olivia—and a year after that they had another daughter, Chloe.

Their family was complete.

Hunter no longer worked all the hours God gave. He was a family man now, very proud of his children and his wife, and Keisha had never been happier. It had been a long haul, and there had been lots of heartache along the way, but it was all forgotten.

Even Hunter couldn't believe that at one time he had actually been thinking of shutting Keisha out of his life. What a mistake that would have been! She was his one true love.

Now and for always!

0807/01a

MILLS & BOON

MODERN

On sale 7th September 2007

BLACKMAILED INTO THE ITALIAN'S BED
by Miranda Lee

Jordan had struggled to forget Gino Bortelli. Now the sexy
Italian was determined to have Jordan in his bed again –
and to her shame, she wanted that too...

THE GREEK TYCOON'S PREGNANT WIFE
by Anne Mather

Greek tycoon Demetri Souvakis needs an heir, and fast, so
demands a divorce from Jane. But before it's final, he'll take
her to bed – for old times' sake, of course...

INNOCENT ON HER WEDDING NIGHT
by Sara Craven

Laine waited for her husband on their wedding
night, knowing their marriage was a sham. When he didn't
come, Laine fled – still a virgin! Now Daniel wants the
night that should have been his...

THE SPANISH DUKE'S VIRGIN BRIDE
by Chantelle Shaw

Ruthless duke Javier Herrera needs a wife.
In Grace Beresford – the daughter of a man who
fleeced Javier of millions – he sees an opportunity
for revenge *and* a convenient wife...

Available at WHSmith, Tesco, ASDA, and all good bookshops
www.millsandboon.co.uk

0807/01b

MILLS & BOON

MODERN

On sale 7th September 2007

THE MEDITERRANEAN BILLIONAIRE'S SECRET BABY
by Diana Hamilton

Francesco Mastroianni's affair with Anna was cut short
when her father tried to blackmail Francesco. Seven months
later, he is shocked to see Anna – struggling to make
ends meet and visibly pregnant!

THE BOSS'S WIFE FOR A WEEK
by Anne McAllister

Spence Tyack needed a wife for a week... It seemed
his demure personal assistant Sadie would take the role –
and not only was she sensible in the boardroom, she
was sensual in the bedroom!

THE KOUROS MARRIAGE REVENGE
by Abby Green

Kallie knew love had nothing to do with her marriage to
Alexandros Kouros. Alex would have revenge for the
mistake that had shattered both their pasts when he
took her as his arranged bride...

JED HUNTER'S RELUCTANT BRIDE
by Susanne James

When wealthy Jed Hunter offers Cryssie a job as his
assistant, she has to take it: she has a sick sister to provide for.
Soon Jed demands Cryssie marry him – it makes good
business sense. But Cryssie's feelings run deeper...

Available at WHSmith, Tesco, ASDA, and all good bookshops
www.millsandboon.co.uk

0807/06

MILLS & BOON
MODERN
Extra
On sale 7th September 2007

STEAMY SURRENDER
by Ally Blake

Morgan had come from Paris to see her inheritance
for herself – a row of shops in a Melbourne suburb.
Their spokesman was millionaire gelateria owner
Saxon Ciantar, and he made certain she knew where she
stood: she was their evil landlady and they were at war!
But Saxon soon began to see glimpses of the real Morgan
– and then he decided that he would fast-thaw the
ice maiden with his searing touch!

DREAM JOB, HOT BOSS!
by Robyn Grady

Working in Sydney's most dynamic advertising agency,
Serena Stevens is in heaven! And she's just landed the
agency's biggest account – this will make or break her
career... Serena's sexy boss, Australia's top tycoon
David Miles, may be all business in the boardroom,
but soon he is loosening his tie...and he wants a little
business in the bedroom! Before long Serena has
to choose...her dream job versus her hot boss!

Available at WHSmith, Tesco, ASDA, and all good bookshops
www.millsandboon.co.uk

Mediterranean Men

Let them sweep you off your feet!

Gorgeous Greeks
The Greek Bridegroom by Helen Bianchin
The Greek Tycoon's Mistress by Julia James
Available 20th July 2007

Seductive Spaniards
At the Spaniard's Pleasure by Jacqueline Baird
The Spaniard's Woman by Diana Hamilton
Available 17th August 2007

Irresistible Italians
The Italian's Wife by Lynne Graham
The Italian's Passionate Proposal by Sarah Morgan
Available 21st September 2007

www.millsandboon.co.uk   M&B

FREE

4 BOOKS AND A SURPRISE GIFT!

We would like to take this opportunity to thank you for reading this Mills & Boon® book by offering you the chance to take FOUR more specially selected titles from the Modern™ series absolutely FREE! We're also making this offer to introduce you to the benefits of the Mills & Boon® Reader Service™—

- ★ **FREE home delivery**
- ★ **FREE gifts and competitions**
- ★ **FREE monthly Newsletter**
- ★ **Books available before they're in the shops**
- ★ **Exclusive Reader Service offers**

Accepting these FREE books and gift places you under no obligation to buy; you may cancel at any time, even after receiving your free shipment. Simply complete your details below and return the entire page to the address below. You don't even need a stamp!

YES! Please send me 4 free Modern books and a surprise gift. I understand that unless you hear from me, I will receive 6 superb new titles every month for just £2.89 each, postage and packing free. I am under no obligation to purchase any books and may cancel my subscription at any time. The free books and gift will be mine to keep in any case.

P7ZEE

Ms/Mrs/Miss/Mr.......................................Initials ....
BLOCK CAPITALS PLEASE

Surname ....

Address ....

....

....Postcode ....

Send this whole page to:

The Reader Service, FREEPOST CN81, Croydon, CR9 3WZ

Offer valid in UK only and is not available to current Mills & Boon® Reader Service™subscribers to this series. Overseas and Eire please write for details. We reserve the right to refuse an application and applicants must be aged 18 years or over. Only one application per household. Terms and prices subject to change without notice. Offer expires 31st October 2007. As a result of this application, you may receive offers from Harlequin Mills & Boon and other carefully selected companies. If you would prefer not to share in this opportunity please write to The Data Manager at PO Box 676, Richmond, TW9 1WU.

Mills & Boon® is a registered trademark owned by Harlequin Mills & Boon Limited. Modern™ being used as a trademark. The Mills & Boon® Reader Service™ is being used as a trademark.